Published by:
Grand Mal Press
Forestdale, MA
www.grandmalpress.com

Library of Congress Cataloging-in-Publication Data
Grand Mal Press/Thomas, Ryan C.

p. cm

Cover art by Grand Mal Press
www.srbproductions.net

FIRST EDITION

BORN TO BLEED

by
Ryan C. Thomas

GRAND MAL

PRESS

For Gramp

Chapter 1

Do you know what a two-headed camel fucking a rocking chair looks like? I do. It looks like the shitty abstract painting that hangs over my therapist's desk. It's really just a blotch of colors, a glorified Rorschach, but I defy you to see anything else in it. I'd always wanted to tell her what I thought of that painting but found more humor in letting her believe it was a good purchase. If I told her I saw freaky animals and furniture engaged in coital struggles, it would just be overanalyzed and end up in my file. There's already enough weird shit in my file as it is.

The last time I was there, watching that two-headed camel go to town on that chair, it almost made me horny. But mostly it made me angry. I dunno, I was feeling fed up that day and bad art kills me; and bad art that sells makes me want to cry. I should know. I do it for a living. And that certainly doesn't help my depression any.

Dr. Marsh leaned forward on her couch. "Your birthday was yesterday?"

She knew full well when my birthday was; she was just trying to open up a new line of questioning. I don't know what she thought she'd get from talking about my age. Maybe she thought I'd gained some maturity points in the last few days. Maybe she wanted to test my age-to-wisdom ratio. I had no idea how old she was, but I doubted it was more than five years more than me. Whatever, I obliged her. "Yeah. Thirty years old."

"Feel any different?"

"No."

"Feel more adult?"

Depends. Do adults get jealous of things that fuck rocking chairs? I shook my head. She kept staring at me, her eyes almost sad, as if she were looking at a puppy. If I didn't say something she'd keep pestering. "Not really. When my mom turned thirty, she seemed a lot . . . older. I don't feel old. Kind of feel like a kid, still. Is that weird?"

"Oh, I don't think so. Times have changed. Thirty is the new twenty. Plus your mom had children so her mindset was different. She was responsible for you and your sister's lives. That makes people grow up pretty quick."

The mention of my sister cut through me, made me look at the ground. It was an involuntary response, as if I might be able to remove myself from the room by staring down through the carpet. I didn't like talking about Jamie and Dr. Marsh knew that. I couldn't tell if she did it on purpose or if she'd forgotten. Part of me wanted to yell at her, but I wasn't about to lose my cool here.

"Do you want kids?" she asked.

Oh, for the love of . . . . We'd been over this before. She was like a broken record. "Someday. Maybe. I dunno."

She scribbled something on her legal pad. She was always taking notes during our conversations. I can't imagine what they amounted to. Roger Huntington, thirty years old, might want kids, has the personality of a sock, seems way too interested in that painting over my desk . . .

She put the pen in her mouth and sucked on its end for a minute. Freud would have been proud of where my mind went. "What have you been doing with your free time? Any dates recently?" Only with porn sites and an Xbox console.

My life was pretty boring, but Dr. Marsh and I had discussed my tendency to be negative so I decided not to get into it. Maybe that's weird. I guess you're supposed to tell your shrink about your pathetic nights alone looking at HotCollegeChicksInHeat.com, but I wasn't up for the spelunking she'd do inside my brain if I did. "No. Don't meet many girls."

"What about that one at the gallery? What was her name?"

I hesitated. "Victoria."

"Yes . . .Victoria. Do you talk to her?"

I nodded. "She works there. I sell there. See her sometimes."

"You like her?"

"I guess."

"Roger, you'll never know if you don't take a chance. Are you afraid of the rejection?"

I shrugged. Who isn't afraid of rejection?

"I mean, if that's what's holding you back, then you're going to go through life alone and miserable. You've got to stop hiding in this shell you've created and start talking to people. That's when the healing will really start."

Then what am I paying you for, I thought, to test steno pads? "Doesn't matter. She has a boyfriend. Gabe something."

Dr. Marsh set her pad and pen down on the couch cushion next to her. Unlike some shrinks, Dr. Marsh preferred to use two couches——one for her and one for her patients. I think she felt it leveled the playing field. All it really did was make the whole process look unprofessional. I mean, you go to a shrink, you expect to lie on a couch while some twat in tortoise shell glasses analyzes your dreams from a leather chair. You don't expect to sit across from each other like it's a frickin' tea party. Times have changed. Except for the part about dissecting my dreams. She was always asking about my nightmares. But, you know, since they *were* a big part of my issues, I guess I couldn't blame her for practicing some archaic therapy.

"Roger, don't tell anyone I told you this, but unless a girl is married—and even then sometimes, but that's not the point—she can be swayed. I think you should give it a shot. Who knows? Maybe she hates the guy but is too codependent to end it."

She was analyzing people she didn't even know. Brilliant. She might as well have her own talk show and commune with people's dead grandparents.

"Maybe."

"Do you want her?"

In the worst way. But I didn't say this; I just nodded. I'd become a professional nodder these last few years. You'd be amazed at how much easier it is than talking, and most people prefer it. Saves them the trouble of having to politely probe for conversation. You nod, they nod back, you each move on.

She picked up her pad again and scribbled something, maybe her grocery list for all I knew. "How have the nightmares been?"

Ah, now we were getting into that twat zone. My dreams. My nightmares. The only thing I could count on these days. Last night's dream had been bad, waking me up in a sweat, but still not the worst

I've had. Some nights I wake up screaming. Some nights I find myself in the kitchen, disoriented and shaking. Sometimes I'm holding a knife and crying. My left thumb has a nice scar on it from one of my somnambulistic episodes. I almost severed it off into my fish tank.

If you want to know what my dreams really consist of—the blood, the rituals, the screams and pleas for help—you'll have to read Dr. Marsh's notes. I tend to forget them after I relay them to her. Sort of like a purging function. Once they're out, they're out. The stronger ones that linger are overwritten by the next terrible nightmare anyway so . . . I almost didn't want to get into last night's with her, but I knew she'd keep pushing if I resisted.

"Did you dream last night?" she said.

"Yes," I replied.

"About the man?"

Yeah, about the man. She didn't need to say his name, didn't need to describe him. We both knew who the man was.

"If you don't tell me we can't put it behind us," she said. "Come on, spill it. We need to do this."

We? Right. She liked to think she and I were some team going through this together. She might have known my past, but she knew absolutely nothing about the reality of that summer ten years ago. She and I were *not* a team; she was not ever going to empathize with me no matter how hard she tried. If I could take her back to those few days in the mountains and put her in that freak's cellar, chain her to the wall next to Tooth and me, she wouldn't be patronizing me now. She'd be drooling in a corner begging for death. And yet, she'd come highly recommended by my old counselor in New Hampshire. She was an expert with trauma victims, or so he'd said. If Tooth was here he'd just say she had nice tits and wasn't too old for a late night fuck.

I could hear his voice now: *Dude, you don't have to talk to her, just stick it in her mouth, gag her with your sack, and then let's go grab a brew.*

"Yeah," I replied. "He was sitting in my car with me, the man. We were smoking weed and he asked me to go to a party with him and I said okay."

"And you feel regret for saying okay?"

"I guess."

"Then what happened?"

I reached up and adjusted the Red Sox cap on my head. My finger brushed the ripped cloth of the brim and I reminded myself I'd have to sew it up soon before it fell to tattered ribbons.

"He lit a cigarette. We just looked out the windshield at this empty street. There was a girl walking across it. Young, in jeans and a tank top. He laughed, got out of the car and started walking toward her and . . ." I hung my head. It was pointless to relive that dream. They were all some iteration of a fucked up bloodbath anyway, so I'm sure Dr. Marsh knew how it would end. They always ended the same way. I looked at the floor again.

"He killed her," she said.

I continued to study the carpet. Of course he killed her. She knew that.

"Okay. You can stop if you want," she said. "Do you want to?"

"Yeah."

"Okay. Well, our time is almost up anyway. It's just a dream. It's your subconscious dealing with stress. You know that. We've talked about it. You spend all day every day thinking about this stuff and it builds up in your brain. Try this for the next week. Think about that girl Victoria. I bet you'll have better dreams." She smiled in a weird sexually suggestive way. A shudder ran down my back. "And try to let go of your cynicism. I feel you getting a bit more pessimistic these days. You seem more down than the last time we met."

I'd been tortured, chained up, brutalized, and forced to watch my sister and best friend die under a maniac's ax blade. How do you get it across to some people that you simply have little belief in the benevolence of humankind? Being angry was all I had these days, because how else could I deal with ten years of regret and night-terrors? It was the only feeling I'd developed in the last decade that felt comfortable.

But I knew she was right, even if I didn't want to admit it. "I'll try."

I got up and put my zippered hoodie on while Dr. Marsh rattled on about needing to meet a half hour later next week. I wanted to tell her that in fact I wouldn't be back next week, but I didn't want to get into it in person. I had decided on the drive over this would be my last session. The nightmares would never end, and this was costing too much money as it was. I'd lived with the bad dreams for this long, I could go another twenty years, I guessed. I was content being messed up and cynical.

I stopped as I opened the door to the common room, turned around and looked at her. She was rifling through papers on her desk. "I'm not afraid of him," I said.

She studied me for a second, then reached for her pad again. But I shouted, "No!"

She tensed up, kind of froze. It was the first time I'd seen Dr. Marsh scared. Scared of me. Mind you, my intent was not to scare her; I just didn't want to watch her write as I talked. It's fucking annoying. I wanted to see her eyes. She glanced quickly at the telephone on her desk, maybe gauging how fast she could call security. How's that for gratitude. She pretends to be my friend for a year, but at the end of the day, I'm just another freak with a potential anger management problem that may or may not do someone real harm one day.

"I'm not afraid of him," I said more firmly. "I let him kill the girl in my dream, then I killed him. That's what I hate. That I let him kill the people in my dreams *first*. I could get him before he does, but I don't. I wait. I always wait. I don't know why, because I'm not afraid of him anymore. I stopped being afraid a long time ago I just…wait."

Dr. Marsh was still on edge. I could tell she wanted me to leave. "We'll discuss it next week, Roger. I have another patient to deal with."

I liked the way she let that slip: "deal with." Just proof that we meant nothing to her, just part of a job that paid her rent. She could deal with my absence from now on.

I pointed to the wall above her desk. "That painting sucks."

I left, and drove to the Robertos near my apartment to get some lunch, had a carne asada burrito but only ate half of it. The first time I had Mexican food in California was a real surprise to me. I mean an eye-opening experience of cosmic proportions. Back home on the east coast Mexican food consists of Taco Bell and frozen burritos you buy at the supermarket. But that's not real Mexican food. Real Mexican food is found at places like Robertos, Aibertos, Titos, etcetera. Little stands on Southern California street corners that serve up made-to-order taquitos, rancheros, chimichangas, burritos, all authentic and covered in fresh guacamole. The taste is from another world. Taco Bell is a travesty by comparison.

I took the remainder of my burrito home to my small studio apartment and put it in the fridge. It would provide good company for the half-empty bottle of ketchup and the two cans of beer that made up the rest of my dietary needs.

My cell phone vibrated in my back pocket. I took it out and looked at the number. It was the gallery. I prayed it was Victoria. "Hello?"

"Roger. What the fuck!" It was Barry Goldstein, gallery owner and pain-in-my-ass extraordinaire. "I thought you said you'd have the paintings to me today. We've got two days before the show. Where are they?"

In the background I could hear Victoria talking to someone. It sounded like she was on her own cell phone. She was giggling and I had a momentary image of me kissing her someday. Yeah, right, as if that would ever happen. I tried to will Barry to put her on the phone, but apparently I don't have the Force.

"They're not done," I said.

"Are you . . . are you fucking with me? Not done? Roger, they need to be framed and lit and hung up! It takes time. How not done are we talking? Half done? Three quarters? What?"

"Not started."

There was silence on the other end of the phone. Then, through forcibly calm breathing, "Roger, if you don't get me those last two paintings by tomorrow morning this show is off and I'll make sure all the other galleries in town know how unreliable you are. Got me?"

I took a nickel out of my pocket and dropped it in the coffee can on my counter. The label on it read Barry's Empty Threats. Trying to scare me was his MO. The guy needed therapy more than I did. He hadn't fired me yet and he never really would because I sold well.

"Roger," he continued, "these are important people who buy this stuff. They're collectors, and they rely on me to get them the product. Some of these people pay very well for what I solicit. And you're not the only artist in town. Understand?"

"So you can get me more money?"

"That's not what I'm saying. What I'm saying is . . . these people
. . . they've got the money to pay for whatever they want. They
could get it elsewhere but they stay with me because I deliver. That's
what I do. Right now they want your work, so I'm giving you my
built-in customer base. But if you waste my time, I can make it so
they don't want your stuff anymore. I can break an artist as easily
as I can make him. I will not deal with your lazy attitude anymore."

"But this is California. Everyone's lazy."

"Stuff your New England east coast bullshit up your ass. If you
don't like it here, then go home and piss in the snow. If you're stay-
ing and you want to get paid, deliver me two fucking paintings by
tomorrow morning!" He hung up.

I put the phone down and leaned against the counter. The com-
ment I'd made about Californians made me smile. I never used to
talk back to people like that. At times it didn't even feel like me; it
felt more like Tooth. Tooth who'd never had a serious thing to say
in his life . . . until that stuff in the basement happened.

I knew I'd gone batshit the first time I caught myself having a
conversation with Tooth in a bookstore at the mall. He kept telling
me books were stupid and I finally told him, "Maybe you should try
reading one instead of using them to kill bugs? You might be enlightened, you ignorant jackhole."

Everyone in the bookstore had stared. Some even moved away
from me. Of course they had good reason to, since Tooth was not
in the store with me. He'd been dead for years at that point. I just
couldn't get him out of my head. I still can't.

I feel him sometimes. I don't know how to explain it. It's like a
haze inside my brain, like I've swallowed his aura. When I'm alone
and I talk to him, his answers don't feel like they come from me.
They're always unpredictable and snarky, which was Tooth's natural way of corresponding, unique only to him. Dr. Marsh says it's a
coping system of mine, which makes sense clinically, but sometimes
I'm not so sure.

I stared at my living room walls where I'd framed and hanged
two paintings I'd done since moving to California last year. One
was of a female assassin, Lena 12, fighting a red-fanged alien with

a sword. I'd painted her in a thong and metal bikini top, her mouth in a tight sneer. The other one was the inside of some industrial machine shop that was an exercise at playing with shadows. In the foreground loomed a giant lathe with a big green button on it that read PRESS TO STOP. I often thought about pressing it, just putting my finger through the painting and seeing what would happen. Would the world go black, would it all just end? It's an enticing thought.

They were good paintings and I was proud of them. Proud that I'd proved my father wrong—I *could* make money being an artist— and proud because I'd sold the image rights to an independent comic book publisher for enough money to buy a six pack of beer and a beta fish. Independent publishing doesn't pay, my friends. But then, pride is worth more in the long run so it evens out.

I tell myself that, anyway.

Thing is . . . these types of paintings were not my bread and butter. Californians don't want dark, sci-fi geekery; they want schlock culled from tropical paradigms, images from films like *Endless Summer* and *Cocktail*. So that's what I paint for money. They call it Plein Air, which stands for open air, meaning you paint outdoors. Really it's just a fancy way of saying "boring landscapes that get old women's panties wet." Long stretches of beach with palm trees blowing in the breeze, waterfalls and rock formations, the occasional woody with a surfboard on top. Collectors hang them up in their game rooms or over their kitchen tables. Hell, you can buy a thousand just like them at Bed Bath & Beyond, but collectors want one-of-a-kind stuff. They want to brag to their guests about how it's an original from a famous local artist and they got it at a gallery show and blah blah blah look at me I'm so important. Little do they know I live in a crappy box of an apartment because what little money I make off those paintings goes toward my shrink bills and car payments on my vintage '82 Camaro. Hey, I'm entitled to a little bit of luxury, right?

The other reason these collectors want originals is because they like to go to the exact spot in the painting and take a photograph. Then they hang the photo next to the painting to prove the scene wasn't just made up. Plein Air collectors are weird, but don't look at me . . . I have aliens on my wall. A quick look outside the window told me I still had the brunt of the day to get the paintings done. My process is simple: scout a location that hasn't been painted before (I'm not the only plein air artist in So Cal), set up my easel so I can get it right, and paint until I'm drunk. The natural lighting really does make a big difference when mixing colors for the final product. And the alcohol makes me not care that I'm painting stuff that would make even Bob Ross groan, were he still alive.

I figured I could get one done this afternoon, albeit sloppily, and take a photo for the next one to do at home tonight. Burn the midnight oil and all that. The lighting would be off but Barry probably wouldn't notice. Only color he really cared about was green, which I don't say to sound like some anti-Semitic jerk. It's got nothing to do with him being Jewish, just with him being an asshole.

I grabbed two canvases, my paints, and those two beers from the fridge and made my way down to the parking lot.

It was almost one in the afternoon. The Clash was on the radio belting out "The Magnificent Seven." I checked my rearview mirror to back out, saw my Red Sox hat looked worse than I'd thought. It was faded and ripped and the red B was starting to unthread. This hat had been through a lot, and it meant a whole bunch to me. Tooth's father gave it to me a few months after the funeral. If Tooth had ever written a will, I'm sure it would have specified he be buried with it (and maybe a beer and some Traci Lords videos, too). It needed a major overhaul. I took it off, mussed my hair, and put it back on, checked the rearview mirror and froze.

The man from my dreams was looking at me from the backseat, his gaunt, unshaven face stained in blood. He held up a bloody fishing gaff and said, "Bet you didn't know I raped Jamie with this for a whole hour. She weren't no virgin when I was done with her. I covered it in Butch's dog shit first. Oh yeah. And when I yanked it out all sorts of good stuff spit out at me. That fucking bitch came, I swear." He laughed that high-pitched witch's cackle, the same laugh that haunted my dreams every night.

I closed my eyes and gripped the steering wheel so hard my knuckles popped. You might be thinking I said something like "I know you're not real," like some lame movie cliché, but I didn't. Because I'm not afraid anymore. I said, "When I open my eyes, if you're really there, I'm going to rip your fucking head off, reach down your throat and tear your lungs out."

I opened my eyes. He was gone. Another hallucination. I'd been off my meds for a month now and Dr. Marsh said some old symptoms might reoccur. It's classic post traumatic stress disorder, or so she said. Same as the war veterans get. It's no fun, let me assure you. Dr. Marsh advised me not to stop taking the pills, but I wanted to try, just to see if I could move past them. Not to mention they were expensive.

I started the car and left, the two cans of beer tapping together on the passenger seat. One for me, and one for Tooth. Only I'd have to drink Tooth's for him. I knew he'd want me to.

Chapter 2

I needed to stop by Murray's Art Depot on Franklin Ave. to re-
stock a few oil paints. It's a small mom-and-pop business with tons
of brushes and paints and canvases and anything else a true starving artist could want. Unlike the big chain stores like Michaels, they
really know their shit. I mean, real artists do not shop for supplies
in places where the majority of aisles are dedicated to scrapbook-
ing. The way those sagging, old women cluck for that stuff you'd
think they were pigs in a feed store. "Oh my gosh, Hazel, did you
see the cute little bunny stickers they have! I'm going to do a whole
new scrapbook of just bunny pictures! Wee!"

The third World War will start over who gets the last bunny
stickers for a scrapbook . . . mark my word.

When I got to Murray's, Cameron Plimpton (Murray's kid) was
working the counter. He looked up from whatever he was reading
when the bell over the door jingled.

"Hey, Roger. Hail to the King, baby."

"Klatu, Verata, Nikto," I replied, our own little joke that drove
his father nuts. Cam was in high school, but he was a pretty cool kid.
He reminded me of me ten years ago, swept up in comics, always
on the lookout for the next great horror film or anything starring
the amazing Bruce Campbell. (Thank God the Academy finally recognized him.)

"You need some paints to do another faggy palm tree picture?"

"You know it."

"You should paint big ol' buttholes on them so your clients can
screw them. Ha!"

"Cam!" Murray came out of the small room behind the counter
where he kept a small fridge and a TV. "What did I say about that
kind of talk when you're working. Hi, Roger."

"Hi, Murray."

Murray grabbed his son by the back of the neck in a loving fatherly way that meant he was two seconds away from grounding the kid for his own good. "I hear you spout anymore homophobic bullshit in this store you're gonna work for free. I'm not gonna lose customers because of your ignorance."

"I'm just joking, Dad. Don't go all Palpatine on me."

"I don't know what that means. Is he mocking me, Roger?"

I laughed. "Not really. Well, maybe. Emperor Palpatine was the ruler of the galaxy in the *Star Wars* films."

Murray cocked an eyebrow. "I'm gonna bet the guy was bad. What happened to kids respecting their parents?"

"Shit, Dad, it's just a joke."

"And no more swearing!"

"But you said 'bullshit.'"

"I said enough. What do you need, Roger?"

"Just need some oils. I know where they are."

"Hold up," Cam said, "I'll come with you. I wanna show you my new stuff." He picked up a sketchpad from next to the register and hopped over the top of the counter. Murray rolled his eyes and went back to watching TV.

Cam and I walked to the paints and I started looking through the various tubes for the colors I needed. I noticed the prices had gone up since I had been here last, but I kept my disappointment to myself.

"Hey, you get the new Batman/Green Lantern mash-up?" Cam asked, flipping through his pad.

"Of course. Got the limited edition foil cover ones as well."

"That was badass when they fought. I thought Batman would kick Jordan's butt, but man oh man he got served."

"All a misunderstanding, anyway. You knew it had to be. They'll never really have two superheroes be enemies for long. Heroes have to stay heroes."

"Oh, here's what I'm looking for. Check this one out," Cam said, offering the sketchpad to me. He was a pretty good artist, dare I say better than I was at his age. On the page was a charcoal sketch of a naked girl with some kind of space gun riding a giant dick and fighting off what looked like more giant dick monsters. As a testament to his skill it was good stuff. As a testament to his hormonal urges, it was scary.

"See, each cock monster shoots sperm grenades and their balls have afterburners in them. She's gotta shoot them in the big vein running down the center to kill them."

"You've got issues," I said.

"Okay okay, that one's just a joke. Seriously, what about this one?" He flipped the page. This new drawing was better, done in colored pencil. A woman in a red bodysuit riding on top of a giant alligator. In the sky, spaceships dueled with lasers. A large red planet shimmered behind the distant clouds. Some kind of sci-fi-fantasy hybrid. It reminded me of a Borris Vallejo book cover.

"That's not bad. Have you tried to enter it anywhere? There are websites you could put it up on and maybe make a sale."

"Not yet. I want to mess with the colors a bit more." He flipped through some more pages and I caught the *Lena 12* comic book in between them. That's the one I did the cover for, the same painting of the female assassin that's hanging in my apartment. I'd signed the copy for Cam a few months ago. It made me feel good to know someone appreciated my geek art. He kept flipping.

"This one here," he said, "I just started yesterday. I'm going to do a big whole ocean battle scene over here. Add some hot mermaids and stuff. But what do you think so far?"

"I like the woman riding the shark. Do you ever have animals that aren't mounted by half-naked women?"

"Well, sometimes they're fully naked. Tits, ass, and big fucking guns, right? Just like you draw."

"Like me? My young padawan, all I do is palm trees."

"Yeah, but you drew Lena 12. She's hot. And deadly. But mostly hot. Really hot. I mean, damn, if I could fuck that—"

The bell over the front door jingled. "Shit," Cam said, "frigging customers."

"It's cool. I'm done. I'll just get these four here." I held up the tubes of paint.

"C'mon, I'll ring you up."

I followed Cameron back to the counter and glanced at the door to see who'd come in. It was a tall brunette girl, maybe in her mid-twenties. She was cute, had a beret on. Cameron was eyeing her as well. He puffed out his chest a bit like a rooster.

For a moment I debated taking Dr. Marsh's advice and trying to talk to her, maybe even use my upcoming gallery show as a way to impress her, but I decided not to. I have no real understanding of how girls work. I had one girlfriend right before I left New Hampshire. The sex was great—I wish Tooth had been around to celebrate with me—but ultimately she couldn't deal with my past.

No one really can. At first they say, "I'm here for you. I understand." But they never do. Then, when I wake up screaming and punching the air with all my might, yelling for someone to leave Jamie alone . . . then they realize they've underestimated how broken I am.

Too bad; this girl was a looker.

"Yo, Iron Man, you doing cash or debit?"

I handed Cam my debit card and he ran it through the reader. The girl made her way up to the counter next to me, stood to my right and smiled. I smiled back. "Hi," she said.

"Hi."

Good so far. Then my palms got sweaty. I dug down deep for something witty to say. "Hi," I repeated, like a moron.

She nodded. And I knew what that meant. She thought I was retarded.

I had nowhere to go from hello. I tried again to think of something clever to say but all I got out was, "Like art?"

Fucking moron. Real smooth. She's in an art store, of course she likes art.

"Sure," she said.

Cameron was trying to hide his embarrassed smile by looking down. The bastard was amused by the way I was crashing and burning. Then what did he do? He cock-blocked me!

"I draw, and you're a hottie. I could draw you on, like, a giant frog or something, in a bikini waving a battle ax."

She actually laughed. This kid had much better game than me. "Thank you," she replied, "I've always wanted to ride on a frog, but I don't really want warts."

Cameron handed me my bag of paints. "Just an urban legend, the warts thing," I said, hoping for another laugh. She just stared at me. Someone kill me.

"Roger here is the real artist," Cameron said, finally coming to my rescue. "Look." He took out the *Lena 12* comic and showed her the cover. "He painted that. Fucking cool, huh?"

"Cam!" This from Murray in the back room.

"It's good," she said, politely, though I could tell she was one of those girls that thought comics were for kids. "But I'm not here to model. My husband and I just bought a condo and we want to stencil the trim. Do you have stencils here?"

I glanced down and saw the ring on her finger. Shit. They were all taken. Just as well. I'd have scared her off soon enough anyway.

"Yeah, over here." Cameron hopped over the counter again.

"Cam! Go *around* the counter!" Murray again.

I said bye to Cam and left him to woo his married frog-riding warrior princess.

Parking on Franklin Ave. is a real bitch. You have to be lucky enough to find a meter on the road, which is nigh impossible on a Saturday afternoon, so I'd parked up a residential side street earlier. The air was pretty warm so the walk back didn't bother me. Not like in New Hampshire. February in So Cal gets as cold as sixty degrees during the day. In New Hampshire it's almost negative sixty. I wasn't missing it much.

There was a dog near my car. A German Sheppard. It wasn't wearing a collar.

I stopped a few yards away and watched it sniff around my tires. My muscles tensed and images of a bloodied Rottweiler flashed through my mind. "What do you want, boy?" I whispered to no one. Dogs and me do not get along for reasons you'll have to talk to Dr. Marsh about. That summer long ago left a pretty dry taste in my mouth for most animals that eat meat.

The dog took a whiz on my back tire and turned around to find me watching. Tentatively, it lowered its head and took a step toward me. The bag fell from my hand as I balled up both fists. The dog took another step, sizing me up.

"If you're gonna do it just do it, fucker." My biceps flexed, my eyes locked on the approaching animal. "Just know it'll be the last thing you ever do."

It was close now, a few feet away, head still down. A debate rang out in my mind whether to rush it or wait for it to rush me. Instead, I stood still, fists at my side. My knuckles cracked.

The dog took four more steps, right up to me, sniffed my shoe. I felt like a slingshot pulled all the way back, waiting to snap. A second passed. Then another. Then, it looked up, kind of smiled the way dogs do, and licked my tight, white knuckles. *Must be the sweat,* I thought. *It likes the taste of my sweat.*

Dr. Marsh's words echoed through my head. Bad dogs are made by humans, they're not born that way. Either that or they're afraid for some reason.

Was Skinny Man made bad, I'd wanted to ask back? Was he afraid of something? No, that sick fuck had been born bad. And there were more of his kind in the world, I knew. Some things are just born evil.

The dog's tongue began to tickle the back of my hand. Slowly, I relaxed, knelt down and got face-to-face with it. I didn't know if it would suddenly turn on me and bite, but I didn't care. Why I test myself in these situations is beyond me, but I have to do it. I have to know I'm truly not afraid, not just spouting off tough words.

The dog licked my face. Its hot breath swam up my nose.

"You're a good boy," I said, and ran my arms around its neck, gave it a playful hug. "A good boy."

"Bogart! Bogart! Leave him alone."

Over the dog's head I could see a man in shorts and sandals heading my way. He jogged over and grabbed the dog by the scruff of the neck and yanked it away from me like he was starting a lawn mower. The poor dog let out a terrified squeak as it was briefly lifted off its front paws. Instinctively, I balled my fists again. This guy's roughness was setting me off.

"Sorry," he said, "he gets out of the yard sometimes. He's harmless though."

Can't imagine why he runs away, I thought. But I said nothing. Just nodded.

"C'mon, Bogart, stupid dog, c'mon." He began dragging the dog back down the street, its paws fighting to get a footing. "Bad dog." He gave Bogart a smack on the ass that elicited another yelp. They disappeared into one of the nearby houses.

"Good boy," I whispered, as if Bogart might hear me on the wind and get some encouragement from it.

My fists uncurled, and now I could hear the plastic bag with my paints whip-snapping in the breeze. Despite wanting to go have a talk with Mr. Animal Lover, it reminded me I had to get a move on or I'd be painting in the dark. And despite the warm weather during the day, the temperature does drop at night in So Cal and all I had on was my sweatshirt.

When I got back in the car, I checked the rearview mirror for my boogey man, but all I saw was the car parked behind me.

Chapter 3

Over the past year, whenever I drove through the county, I kept an eye out for places to paint, so I knew of a spot out east: a small lake ringed with palms that was about ten miles into the desert past the Borengo Casino. I'd actually stumbled upon it while answering a call for local artists the casino put in the paper. They held an art fair every year and the winner got $5,000 and a free buffet at the casino hotel. I hadn't won because I'd brought some small pieces of horror movie icons I'd hybridized with X-Men characters: Wolverine as Freddy Kreuger, Jason Voorhees as Spider-Man, The Bride of Frankenstein as Storm—that kind of stuff. I didn't win, but I sold them for twenty bucks a piece to some college kids who thought they were cool.

Oh, and when I say I'd stumbled onto the lake I mean I'd found it thanks to some poor directions from the Spanish-speaking owner of an avocado stand a few miles south of the casino. Couldn't blame him, really. My thick New Hampshire accent confuses most people I meet out here, let alone anyone who already struggles with English. Thank God my cell phone has a built in GPS and I was able to backtrack to the casino.

The lake's name was Corazon del Agua—Heart of Water. Not very imaginative, but my guess was the early Mexicans named it that more for descriptive purposes than poetry. I knew how to find it well enough. I'd been meaning to do a piece on it for a while now, because the contrast of the desert beyond the lake would be a nice change from the ocean images that usually formed my horizons.

As I got on the highway to head east, my cell phone rang. It was an old friend. "Hola, Officer Teddy. Or should I say, 'Sheriff Teddy'? My dad told me about your promotion."

"Yeah, thanks. 'Bout time I got recognized around here. Plus the bum shoulder makes it hard to drive around and write traffic tickets anyway, so I think they just wanted to put me behind a desk."

"Still hurts you?"

"That dog fucked up all my nerves, but you know this. How's life in California?"

"Well, it's February and I'm only in a hoodie. Could be worse."

"What I wouldn't give. And let me guess, girls in bikinis everywhere?"

"That part of the myth is a lie. No girls in bikinis rollerskating down the 5. They wouldn't get through the traffic jams anyway."

"Well, wait 'til summer, then send me some photos. We all envy you back here, you know. Shit, if I didn't have a wife and kids I'd move out there, too. I'm freezing my nuts off here. They're so cold they're cracking like the frigging Liberty Bell."

"Very patriotic. Should paint 'em red, white, and blue."

"They're already blue. I'm married, remember. Listen, real reason I'm calling is because some website named Thrill of the Kill has been calling your parents' house."

"Crap. Thought my dad changed the number again."

"He did. But these sensationalist pricks always track it down somehow. I ran into your folks at the supermarket and your mom started crying when she told me. I told her I'd find them and lock 'em up for a night or two. Of course, for all I know they're in Canada or something. Anyway, my guess is they'll be calling you at some point so . . . well, you know. Might want to change your number, too." I sighed, sped up around the puttering VW Bug in front of me. "Actually, let them call. I'll tell them what I think of them."

"Yeah, but remember what happened when that Court TV show interviewed you. The whole town ended up looking like a Charlie Manson convention. All they want to hear about is the . . . the . . ."

Sheriff Teddy (then Officer Teddy) had been the first one on the scene that summer ten years ago. He'd been driving past Skinny Man's house and found me covered in blood in the middle of the street, kneeling over a corpse. In fact, he'd almost shot me on sight, thinking me some drugged up homicidal maniac. Thankfully he'd noticed the cuffs on my ankles and the cuts and bruises all over me, and knew things weren't as they seemed. He was a smart cop.

And then Butch, that big Rottweiler, had come out of nowhere and chomped down on Teddy's shoulder.

"The blood," I finished for him. "I know. I've dealt with it before."

"The world is sick, Roger. People get off on this shit. You know I've had a couple of high schoolers here ask to see our family album? Said they were doing a report on the reality of *CSI* episodes."

"What's the family album?"

"It's our book of crime scene photos. It's not pretty."

"Pictures of Jamie in there?" I'm not sure why I asked it; it just came out.

There was silence on the other end. Then: "Yeah. Sorry. I'd burn them if the State would let me. No one deserves to see her like that. No one. She was a cute kid, growing up to be a beautiful girl."

Suddenly I saw an image of Jamie chained to a dirt floor. She'd been beaten senseless and ripped apart by a number of sharp instruments. She struggled to breathe but much of her face had been cut off so all that came out was a bubbling sound. It was a real memory, I knew, but somehow new to me, long buried in my subconscious. Right now, thinking of it as a photograph in some police department three-ring binder, it made me angry. I saw myself looking down at her and crying. Suddenly I wanted to punch something. I wanted to find Skinny Man and beat the shit out of him because I wasn't afraid anymore. I wasn't afraid! I wasn't afraid!

"I'm not afraid of you!"

"Whoa, Roger, you okay?"

I pulled the phone away and looked at the LED. What the hell was I doing? Losing my mind, that's what. "Sorry. Yeah, um . . . just . . . um . . ."

"Hey, no need to explain. I understand."

I doubted he did. Nobody had ever understood. And even though Teddy had been there and seen the carnage, he hadn't lived it like me.

"Okay, well, anyway, I just wanted to touch base and warn you that the self-proclaimed media is still after you. Maybe just screen your calls for a bit."

"Thanks. I appreciate it."

"No sweat. Hey, send some pics back this way of girls in bikinis, even if you have to paint them yourself."

"You got it."

We said goodbye and I drove in silence for a little while. It annoyed me that my history was of so much interest to people. You can find various renditions of what went down that summer on a bunch of websites and even in some true crime books. I'm quoted in some of them, and in others they simply made up what they wanted me to say. It's all romanticized in the end, just like war. But any war veteran who's been in the shit will tell you there's nothing romantic about watching your buddy's leg get blown off.

Or eaten by a Rottweiler.

And then there was Jamie, back in my mind again, dredged up thanks to Teddy's phone call. A faded memory of us at a donut shop, the one Dad used to take us to on Sunday mornings. I always got the jelly-filled ones and she got the ones with chocolate sprinkles. The three of us would sit and eat, Dad reading the paper, Jamie and I making faces at each other. We'd always take an éclair home for Mom.

Jamie later gave up on chocolate when she was thirteen, afraid to get acne. Something she read in a teenie bopper magazine.

I felt my chest growing tight. Think of something else, Roger.

My iPod was in the center console so I took it out and played some tunes. The Beastie Boys, The Dead Kennedys, Guns N' Roses, Nirvana, even a song from the *Star Wars* soundtrack. I sang along, finally letting go of my thoughts, pretending I was on stage at Madison Square Garden.

Traffic, as usual, was moving at a snail's pace. Everyone was bumper-to-bumper and trying to cut each other off as if it would make a difference to be in another lane. I was still a few miles from the turn off toward the casino, after which I'd still have to drive for about fifteen minutes through the back roads.

I know what you might be thinking—that the lake is secluded and no one would hear me scream if I got attacked by a mountain lion or something. But that's not true. I'm not stupid. The access road continues around the entire lake and makes a big loop. There are picnic benches and trash barrels on the far side and a lot of people camp out there. There's also a main road that runs by it on the east side, an alternative route to the casino that is heavily trafficked. It's a fairly popular spot.

Then again, I'd been feeling different lately. I almost wished it was secluded. And I wish Skinny Man was there, just he and I. Yeah, it's messed up, but sometimes I wish I could relive those days in his cellar. I wish I could go back as me now, as the me that was born after I got out of the hospital, because I know Jamie and Tooth would still be here. I wouldn't have run away, wouldn't have hid, wouldn't have cried and peed myself. That Roger Huntington is long dead. Of course Skinny Man's dead, too, so I may as well fight a telephone pole. Man, maybe I do need more therapy.

I crept along for another five minutes and my phone rang again. The number for the gallery was displayed on the LED. I wondered what Barry wanted now.

"Barry?"

"Hi, Roger, it's Victoria."

"Shit!" I slammed on the brake as the car in front of me suddenly stopped short. I flew forward but snapped back thanks to my seatbelt. This is a common occurrence on the Southern California freeways. Someone slows down up ahead and it creates a chain re-action of rapid deceleration until some sap who's not paying atten-tion rear-ends the guy in front of him. It's one reason the traffic is always fucked up—everyone is always crashing into each other like retards.

"Roger? You okay?"

"Yeah. I almost nailed the guy in front of me." For some rea-son that sounded like a bad thing to say to the girl I had the hots for. I could hear Tooth making fun of me. *I bet you wouldn't even give a reach around either, gayboy.* "I mean, with my car," I explained.

She ignored any double entendres and asked, "Where are you?"

"Driving out to BFE to please your boss."

"Aw, look at you, always the nice guy. And here Barry is always cursing you out. I think you get a bum rap, *mon amor.*"

My heart nearly stopped at her flirty French love reference. I knew she was just being funny, because that's how she was. And that's why I loved her from afar. She was the kind of girl that was always smiling, always finding silver linings in problems, always of-fering a hug to anyone having a bad day. It was *she* who was the nice one, not me. I was just quiet, and somehow seen as timid. I guess to girls that equals nice. But I'm not dumb, I know girls don't want nice guys, they want arrogant badboys.

Not that they wanted mental cases either, and in that sense, I was screwed twice over.

I cleared my throat. "Well, if I don't please him he calls me and ties up my phone so . . ."

"Am I tying you up?" There was a hint of teasing in her voice. Or maybe I was just reading into it because I very badly wanted her to tie me up. Hey, I'm a man after all, right?

Answer smooth, buddy. "You could never tie me up. I mean, I want you to tie me . . . . No! I mean . . . that . . . you can call . . . um . . . "

She giggled. I almost crashed again.

"Listen, the reason I'm calling, Mr. Handsome, is I'm in a heap of shit. I was hanging one of your paintings here for Barry, and I spilled my coffee on it. Barry is fucking flipping out."

"So dab it with a towel and tell Barry to take a pill."

"I did. The towel part, anyway. It's not coming out. It seeped into the painting. Barry says he's gonna make me pay for it. He's such a grouch."

"Yeah, he would, wouldn't he. Put him on the phone."

"Ok, thanks, sweetness. Hang on." There was a brief pause, then she was back. "Ugh. He said he doesn't want to talk to you. Said he's gonna fire both of us, which I don't doubt, and I can barely pay my rent as it is. Not that I really care if I lose this job, but still . . . "

Actually, I cared if she lost her job. She was the only good thing about going to that gallery—besides collecting my money from any sales. Suddenly I had a crazy idea. "Did you take your lunch break yet?"

"I'm just about to."

"Okay, well, hit a drive-thru real fast and then meet me at Corazon del Agua Lake. I'll fix it up and you can bring it back and hang it up."

"Isn't that out by the casino? It's gonna take me forty-five minutes just to get there. Barry will dock my pay."

It would probably take even longer with traffic, I realized. "If he does, I'll pay the difference."

"Roger, I couldn't let you do—"

"I want to. It's okay." Truth was I just wanted to see her, and for as smooth as I was—which is in the realm of tree bark—she probably knew it.

"Okay, but if that happens I'll pay you back later."

I laughed, perhaps a little forcibly to see if I could get her to laugh back. Cheap pickup tricks I'd learned from Tooth long ago. "Then we'll constantly be paying each other back and it'll be a vicious circle."

"Yeah, but you're older, so I'll slip you the money on your deathbed and there will be nothing you can do about it. I win. I rule." She laughed.

I didn't. The mention of my deathbed made me go cold. I'd lain in a hospital bed for days after the events of that summer, wishing I was dead. Jaime's bed in the hospital actually *became* her deathbed. "Sure," I said, back to my one-word answers.

"Okay, I think I know how to get there. I'll leave right now."

"Call me if you get lost."

"Thanks, Roger."

"No problem."

She hung up just as I reached the off-ramp towards the casino. The road turned off into some barren foothills that had been fenced off for whatever reason. A few houses sat back from the road on long dirt driveways. This pretty much summed up the east county: a land still wholly untouched by industry and fortune. Not that it was desolate—a billboard for a new community development greeted people at the exit. Los Puentes something or other. The Bridges of . . . what? There were no bridges anywhere around here. The developers must have thought it was metaphorical, like the homes would be a bridge to a better life. Anyway, the rendering of the soon-to-be-constructed homes looked like shit so I rolled my eyes.

I followed this road for about five or six minutes until I saw that avocado stand on the side of the road. The sign on top was new and announced that you could now get strawberries and oranges there as well. A couple of cars were pulled over and some people were buying some of the produce. The same guy was working there from last time. It's no secret these guys are migrant work-

ers, and whether you agree or disagree on the illegal alien issue
(which I couldn't care less about) you really can't beat the prices.
You can get five avocados for a buck at these types of stands. Com-
pare that to a dollar a pop at the supermarket and you understand
why these little stands stay in business.

Next to the stand was the dirt road that led down to the lake.
The truck in front of me turned down it and kicked up a cloud of
dirt that came through my air vents and made me cough. Probably
the couple inside was going to have a little picnic at the lake.

Thinking of other people's happiness started to bum me out.
Back in New Hampshire, I'd been a loser with the ladies. Never
knew how to talk to them. It took me a long time to realize girls
don't care about Captain America's death or which film version of
Halloween is better (John Carpenter's, thank you. Everything the man
touches turns to gold. *Big Trouble in Little China, The Thing, Escape
From New York*, hell, even *The Fog* is an okay film. I guess the one
clunker is *Ghosts of Mars*, but nobody's perfect).

The dirt road wound down a small incline for about a mile and
stopped at a big unpaved parking lot full of crab grass and weeds.
On the other side of the parking lot was that other road I mentioned, the back alternative route to the casino. Cars were speeding
down it like always, every driver inside bursting at the seams to
throw their money away.

I parked the Camaro and turned off the iPod. Through the
windshield I could see the lake before me like a giant puddle of oil.
The dirt road continued on from the far corner of the parking lot
and wound around the lake to the picnic tables. The truck was
halfway around it now, headed toward the park benches. A couple
of other cars were over there too and I could see one couple sitting
on a blanket and laughing.

"Steve Roger's death was a milestone," I said to no one. "Not
my fault girls don't appreciate superheroes."

I grabbed the paints and beer from the seat next to me and
popped the trunk. From inside it I removed my easel, a canvas and
my digital camera. Lying next to a box of used brushes was the
black case that held my gun. It was a Glock 20 that fired .10mm
rounds. I'd only fired it once since my dad bought it for me, just to
make sure it worked. The guys at the gun range were impressed

with my accuracy and precision.

"Damn, man, you should enter contests," this big, bearded fella had said.

"Or become a sniper," his short, fat friend added. "You're a regular killing machine. Go on with your bad self, Rambo. Hey, I know where some gooks hang out in my neighborhood. Can I hire you? You'd be doing the country a service!"

I'd simply nodded. What else was I supposed to do, explain to them how I'd blown apart some evil dog's head as it tried to kill a cop? Explain to them that I had, in fact, killed before? Tell them that I knew I could shoot them between the eyes from one hundred yards away? They'd just ask me to prove it, and I don't know if I would have cared enough to ignore the challenge.

"Careful, Ross," Beardy'd said to his friend as I brushed past him, "it's the silent ones you gotta watch out for."

Short and Fat Ross stuck his hands up, laughing. "Don't shoot! Don't shoot!" He and his buddy thought they were awful funny. They laughed a laugh that haunted my dreams and made me start to shake a little. You know, like the Joker. Like Skinny Man. If I could trade lives with them for two seconds they wouldn't find homicide a laughing matter.

"'Scuse me," I'd said, finally resorting to stepping around them.

"Sure thing. Wouldn't want to get on someone's shooting spree list. We're just trying to make conversation, buddy. Just telling you you're a good shooter. You don't gotta be an asshole."

"What a prick. Jeez, some people don't know how to take a compliment. Should kick his ass to teach him some manners."

I left without incident, picturing myself swinging an ax into their heads. I was sure I could do it, too. I wasn't afraid of them. I was merely afraid of my thoughts.

Anyway, the gun worked so I'd left the range, cleaned it, and it's been in my trunk ever since. As I stared at it now I couldn't help but think it was always going to be a part of me. I don't know how to explain it, but ever since that first time shooting guns with Tooth, I've always felt better having a gun nearby. Maybe it's just the fact that I know I'm good at it. It's weird, it almost feels like a calling. Oh, I've dwelt on it many times, this whole notion of why I'm still alive, why I made it out of Skinny Man's sadistic terror dome unscathed. I'll always wonder if I was just lucky or if I was meant to get out. When I see this gun, I start to believe I was spared for a reason. What that reason is, I couldn't tell you.

After I slammed the trunk and began hoofing it down a small foot trail to the lake, I realized I could trump Victoria's hypothetical win in our payback game. I fumbled out my cell phone and dialed the gallery. She didn't pick up, which meant she must already be on her way. I left a message: "I'll leave it to you in my will. I win. *I* rule."

Chapter 4

The lake was calm, but what lake isn't? A film of dust from the surrounding desert had settled as a dull skin on the water. I wondered if there were fish in there. No one had any fishing poles so it was either void of life or full of the type of fish you don't eat, stuff like sunfish and minnows.

I found a good spot not far from the parking lot, near some half-dead bushes, and set up my easel. I popped open one beer and put the other on the ground. Mixing the colors took another few minutes and then I set brush to canvas, constantly scrutinizing the scene before me. It was as I'd imagined it: the lake, some California Palms over the park benches, foothills and desert beyond, and a blue sky above it all. It didn't get much cheesier than that. I'd make a good buck off it.

The first beer went down quick, and I began to get a nice buzz. Working outside is pretty peaceful, all told. There's a sense of communion with the land, and you start to notice things you wouldn't if you were just passing by: the way the trees have character, the smell the water gives off, the occasional insect fluttering in a wild flower. Just little things that reassure you the Earth is still moving.

A half hour passed and I had most of the water painted. From there I'd do the dirt and scrub brush that surrounded it. But first I wanted the other beer. As was my ritual, I talked to it. "This one's for you, Tooth. Hope you can taste it, because it's cheap and it tastes like shit. Just like your girlfriends used to say about you."

I popped the tab. It hissed and spit beer all over me. "Sonofa!"

How a beer that had been sitting still on the ground for thirty minutes could do that was beyond me. Maybe Tooth was getting me back. "Great. Just great."

I set it back on the ground and went back to my car to look for a napkin. That's when Victoria's Taurus pulled in next to me. Sitting

next to her in the front seat was her boyfriend, Gabe. A frown
spread involuntarily across my face.

"Roger!" she said, getting out. She opened the back door and
took out the painting she'd spilled coffee on. Gabe got out and
pitched a cigarette into some dry brush. Way to go, Smokey the
Bear. He was wearing a black T-shirt, the sleeves rolled up like a
greaser. Not a bad looking kid, but still not worth Victoria's time if
I had anything to say about it.

"Roger, see. Look what I did. I'm such an idiot." She came
around the car and handed me the painting. There was a large
brown stain in the middle of the sky. "Barry is so on the rag today.
Can you really fix it?"

It wouldn't be easy; I'd have to repaint most of the sky, but I
could pull it off. "Yeah, no problem. Take me about twenty minutes
or so."

Gabe cleared his throat. Victoria grabbed his shoulder and ush-
ered him toward me. "Oh, this is Gabe. My boyfriend. I think I've
told you about him before."

"Yeah," I replied. I put out a hand and we shook. His grip was
tight. Guys will do that sort of shit to test each other, to establish
some messed-up sense of dominance. Tooth was always trying to
crush people's hands. I saw more than a few "tough guys" try to
hide a wince when they shook his hand. Problem is, some guys take
it too far, actually go for some pain. Gabe was teetering on that
fence, the prick. I clenched my jaw and dreamt of hitting him.

"Spill something there?" Gabe said, indicting my *Ghost in the
Shell* shirt with a flick of his head.

"Beer."

"Sweet. Got any more?"

I shook my head. "Sorry, didn't know you were coming."

Victoria gave Gabe a friendly shove. "He showed up right as I
was leaving. He wanted to take me to lunch—"

"But she said she had to come here," he cut her off. "So . . . here
we are." He looked around and readjusted his nuts. "Middle of
fucking nowhere."

"Stop being a douche," Victoria told him.

He pointed past me. "'S'like that lake in that *Creepshow* movie.
Look, there's even a weird film on the water."

My inner geek quivered and I wanted to tell him that the name of the vignette was *The Raft*, based on the short story by Stephen King, but I didn't like him enough to try and impress him. And Victoria most likely wouldn't give a shit.

"Bet there are bodies in there," he continued. "Drug cartel kills, all bloated and skeletal at the bottom."

"You're being morbid, babe." Victoria checked her watch. "Really? Twenty minutes?"

I tapped the painting under my arm. "Time me." I smiled at her and she smiled back. Man, I really wanted to kiss her. Why did she have to bring this putz with her? "C'mon." The napkin could wait, I decided. I waved them over to the easel, took the work-in-progress down and replaced it with the coffee-stained painting.

"Have a sip of your beer?" Gabe asked.

"Yeah, go ahead." I wanted to say no.

He took a long gulp that emptied half the can. Dickhead.

"It's actually a beautiful lake," Victoria said. "I've never stopped here. Some friends used to come here in college and get wasted. I never came. Not sure why."

"To busy studying like a book worm," her boyfriend said. Then to me: "She reads, like, a book a week, if you can believe that."

"What books?" I asked her.

She pushed her hair back over her ears. "Oh, anything. Mysteries mostly. I like Ayn Rand too. You ever read her?"

"I read bits of *Atlas Shrugged*," I replied.

"Yeah? I loved that one."

As I mixed some paint to match the color of the sky in the painting, Gabe took out another cigarette and lit it up. "Please don't have some feminist talk. Ayn Rand should get her ass kicked by a rat monkey."

Ok, at that point I couldn't help it. "Rat monkey? You mean from *Dead Alive*?"

He blew out a cloud of smoke. His eyes lit up. "Shit yeah, I love that movie. You ever see *Bad Taste*?"

"Of course. And *Meet the—*"

"*Feebles*! Yes! I love that movie. Peter Jackson is the man. *Lord of the Rings* and *King Kong*."

"That movie sucked," Victoria said. "The stupid monkey ice

skates? C'mon. The original is so much better."

"You into Carpenter?" I asked Gabe.

"*The Thing*! Fucking love that flick. Best horror film ever made, man."

Suddenly I was having flashbacks of watching that movie with Tooth. Boy, I'd had so many flashbacks today I was beginning to miss my medication. Even worse, I was kind of starting to like this Gabe guy. At least his taste in movies was good.

"I'm getting hungry now," Victoria said. "I may run back to that stand and get some fruit. Want me to get you something, babe?"

Gabe snorted. "Fruit? For lunch? Nah. I'll get a burrito when we get back."

"Suit yourself, babe. Just thought we could still get lunch to-gether."

They way she kept referring to him as "babe" made me jealous. I'd never been with anyone long enough to trade terms of endear-ments. Only thing I could do to make myself feel better was keep on painting. The coffee stain was slowly disappearing. Had Barry not seen it beforehand he'd probably never know it had been painted over. Hopefully he'd leave Victoria alone when she brought it back.

She put a hand on my shoulder. "Roger, you want anything. Or-anges? Strawberries? "

I wasn't very hungry, but for some reason I felt like I should be more gracious than her boyfriend. "Um, maybe just an orange. Hang on, I've got a dollar here somewhere."

She laughed. "Please, like I'm gonna make you pay for an or-ange when you're saving my job. It's on me. I'll be right back. You two can stay and talk about your weird movies."

"Thanks." I smiled. Like an idiot.

She stepped around me and kissed Gabe on the mouth. I spi-raled a bit further into depression. "Love you, babe."

Gabe kissed her back and patted her butt. "Love you too, gor-geous."

It really sank in at that moment that they were in love. It was a strange "opposites attract" kind of love, but you could see it was for real. Clearly she dug his bad boy attitude. Tooth had always had that same kind of "asshole" quality that girls liked. I'll never understand it. She squeezed his hand, then made her way back to her car.

She was genuinely happy with this guy. It made me sad.

As she was pulling out, a muddy SUV passed by her on its way to the other side of the lake. All the windows were down. Arms dangled out of them, attached to cigarettes. The two guys in the front seat, and the one guy in the back seat, all leered down into Victoria's car. I guess attractive girls get that a lot. But for some reason it set me on edge. These guys looked creepy, like the type of guys that hang out in biker bars just looking for trouble. And I mean *real* biker bars, not those hipster dive bars.

Gabe saw it too and actually yelled out to them. "She's taken, assholes!"

The guy in the backseat leaned out and flipped him off as the SUV continued on. Gabe returned the sentiment. For a minute I thought they'd come back and start some shit, but they didn't.

"You get that a lot?" I asked. "People looking at her like that?"

"Fuck. Everywhere we go. I swear I had to start lifting weights just so I could get guys to leave her alone at the bars."

"Well, be glad you have it."

He finished his cigarette and stamped it out. "You go the bachelor route?"

Not by choice, friend. "I guess."

"Don't sweat it. I used to be like that. All I wanted was a good fuck. Nowadays, I dunno . . . Victoria kind of changed me. She says she domesticated me. I told her not to turn me into anything with more than two syllables 'cause it hurts my head."

He laughed at his own joke. I cracked a smile myself.

"But I miss the old days, too. I had a lot of 'tang about two years ago. I fix cars. You know, a mechanic. So I'd trade work for favors sometimes. Don't tell Victoria I told you that."

"Mums the word." Well, at least now I had some ammo to use against him should I desire to break them up. Which, of course, is not how I am. Just wishful thinking and all.

"She gives a hell of a blowjob though. I swear. Sucks my eyeballs into my fucking skull. Don't tell her I told you that either." He paused. "You must get laid a lot doing this shit, huh?" He pointed to the painting.

Why people think artists have girls clamoring for them is beyond me. Unless my fish is female—and I have no idea how to
check so don't ask—there isn't a girl on the planet who gives two
shits about me. The fish only likes me because I feed it. And really,
it has no idea where the food comes from anyway, just that it suddenly appears on top of the water, so even if it is female you can
scratch that notion, too.

"Not really," I replied.

"Why not? Don't girls go all stupid over art and shit? Don't they
all take photos and write poetry and hang up flower prints over
their beds? You telling me no girls are willing to suck you off for a
free painting?"

I wished he'd stop pressing this issue. "Kind of have a . . .
strange history. Most people don't really get it."

"Strange history? What? You on the run or something? Blow up
your high school?"

"Not quite."

"Wait, you're not in the closet are you? That would explain why
Victoria likes you. She's has a couple of gay friends. She's got a fag
hag side to her. Not that I mind . . . I mean . . . if you are." He
paused again. "Fag hag is okay to say, right? It's, like, accepted and
all?"

"I'm not gay, Gabe." I picked up the beer and downed the rest
of it in as manly a way as I could. Even rolled out a low burp just
for his benefit.

"So you're straight?"

I rolled my eyes. "As an arrow."

"Just checking. Like I said, nothing against gay guys . . . but I
never know what to talk about with them. Have some gay guys that
bring their cars to me. Nice guys, actually. You think they like Peter
Jackson films?"

I should introduce this guy to Cam at the art store. They could
both solve the "mystery" of homosexuality, which so far consisted
of trees with assholes in them and ignorance of New Zealand film-
makers.

The coffee stain was completely gone now, so I took the painting off the easel and carried it to my car, placed it in the backseat.
As I went back to work on the previous painting, Gabe picked up

a rock and pitched it into the water. It made a *kerploop*, and the film on the water's surface spread out in a wide circle.

"Want to know the real reason I tried to take Vic to lunch today?" he said.

I finished the top of a palm tree on the canvas before asking, "Why?"

"This." He reached into his pocket and pulled out an envelope. He opened the top and shook the contents out into his other hand. It was a diamond ring. "I'm going to propose."

To say my heart sank would be an understatement, but I didn't want to let on how much I suddenly hated his guts again. Chances are she'd say yes and all my daydreams about going on a date with her would never be anything but that—just daydreams.

"You don't have a box?" I asked.

"I do, but it bulges out in my pocket and I wanted to surprise her. It's a quarter carat, which ain't much, but the guy at the store said we can upgrade over time. Trade it in for a half carat in, like, two years. What do you think?"

I sighed. What could I say? "Think you're one lucky guy."

"Yeah, except now we won't have time to go to lunch." What do you think about doing it here, at this lake? Is that romantic?"

"Spontaneous maybe. Romantic? I dunno. Better than at a Burrito shop though."

"You think?"

"I wouldn't worry about it. She seems to be really into you."

"Well, shit, almost two years now, she'd better be."

I kept on painting, trying my best not to think about it, hoping maybe he'd just put the damn ring away and change the subject. Go back to talking about horror movies and girls who gives blowjobs for oil changes.

He snapped his fingers. "Oh shit. I just had an idea. You could, like, paint a picture of us and we could hang it in our apartment. Would you do that?"

Paint a picture of the girl I had the hots for and her grease monkey husband? Sure, why not. Why should I ever get to paint stuff that actually makes me feel good?

"I mean, I'll pay you. Like, fifty bucks. Is that cool?"

Normally I'd charge about four hundred for a portrait, but I relented since it would be for Victoria. Yeah, I'm a sap. "Sure. I'll need to get a photo of you."

"I think I have one in my wallet." He took it out of his back pocket and rummaged around in it. "Shit. Guess not."

"It's okay. I brought my camera. When she gets back I'll take one—"

"But don't tell her what it's for. I want it to be a surprise. I'm gonna go find a good spot around here to pop the question." He took off toward the water. When he reached the edge of the lake he began walking around the perimeter. Across the water I could see the SUV parked near some picnic tables. Three arms hung out the windows, all smoking cigarettes. Hopefully Gabe wouldn't be stupid enough to walk by them alone. Maybe it wouldn't matter though; there were a handful of couples still laying in the grass, and one guy playing Frisbee with his dog. It was rare you saw three guys beat someone up in broad daylight in front of witnesses.

Of course, Skinny Man had attacked us in broad daylight. So who can say.

Chapter 5

Victoria came back about ten minutes later, parked her car, and walked up to me. She picked a few strawberries out of a little container. "The oranges all looked gross so I spared you. I got these instead. They're super juicy. You want one?"

I shook my head. I hadn't really wanted the orange that much anyway. And I'd since lost my appetite knowing Gabe was about to propose. All I really wanted was another beer. Maybe some weed. And for Gabe to fall in the lake with his ring and drown.

"Hey, did you fix the painting?" she asked.

"Yeah, it's in my car. Hang on." I put my brush down and walked with her to the parking lot.

When she saw the painting she did a little jump. "Oh wow! You can't even tell I spilled on it. Thank you thank you!"

She leaned over and gave me a kiss on the cheek. My face flushed and I felt electricity flow through my body. I'd wanted for so long to feel her lips against me. Her breath smelled of strawberries and she got some of the juice on me but I didn't want to wipe it off. I know, that sounds creepy, but I still felt it there and it was a sweet reminder.

She took the painting and put it in her own car, then checked her watch. "Oh crud, I need to get back before Barry calls me and chews me out. Hey, where's Gabe?"

"He went for a walk over near the water."

"Dammit. He knows I need to get back. Sometimes he's such a retard."

"Yeah, but you love him. Right?" I stressed the last word a bit too much and she cocked her head at me.

"Sure. I love him. Why? He wasn't being a dick or anything while I was gone, was he?"

"No. He . . . he seems like a cool guy."

She smiled, and for the first time I could tell she knew I liked her. I looked away, afraid to meet her eyes. "He comes off like a jackass a lot of the time, I know, but he's always been there when I needed him. Sounds weird, a guy like him and a girl like me connecting, but we do. Trust me, I get it from my parents all the time. They don't get it either, but it's there. He gives me foot rubs, actually asks me how my day was, doesn't complain when I ask him to keep me company at the mall. You know what he did for Valentine's Day? He bought a fondue set and made a bed on the living room floor. We ate and watched Rom Coms all night and just cuddled. He's a sweet guy, once you get past the machismo. Yeah, I love him. More than I've ever loved anyone else. And who knows, maybe I'll even get him to read a book one of these days."

I nodded. Always with the nodding.

Just then Gabe came up the dirt path and stood before us. "'Sup, homies. Ooh, strawberries!" He snatched one from Victoria's container.

"Find what you were looking for?" I asked him.

He put a hand on my shoulder. "I did indeed. You got that camera?"

I walked around the two lovers and motioned them to follow me to the easel. Victoria asked Gabe what he needed a camera for as they pulled up behind me.

"Stand over there." I pointed to the water.

They made their way across a small patch of dirt and ice plant. Gabe put his arm around Victoria.

"Say cheese." I snapped the shot and made sure it was lit okay in the display. Had to admit it was cute, if not heartbreaking for me.

"Why are you making Roger take photos?" Victoria gave Gabe a quick peck on the lips. "Tell me."

"I'm setting up a porn site for us. We need some 'before' photos."

She punched him in the arm. "Stop being gross. Roger?"

Gabe gave me a look that asked me to keep his secret. I shrugged. "Something about a porn site is all I know."

"You guys suck. Whatever. Have your little secrets. I need to head back so I don't get fired."

"No!" Gabe grabbed her by the arm. "We can't go yet."

"Why? You know how Barry can be."

Gabe turned to me. "Yo, Rog, what time does the sun set?"

I looked up at the sky. Probably wouldn't set for another two hours at least. But I knew if I said that Victoria would make him leave and I had a hunch he wanted to propose under a pink sky. Romance and all that. I guess he did have some skills. "Soon," I told him. This guy owed me big time.

"We need to stay just a bit, then." He pulled her into him, kissed her on the lips.

"Gabe! What don't you get? I have to get back."

"I'll take the painting back for you," I told her. She shook her head in confusion and stared back and forth between us.

"Someone tell me what the fuck is up."

It was rare I heard her swear and for some reason it excited me. Guess she had a bad girl side after all. It only made her a little more attractive to me and I was starting to feel pretty depressed over the whole thing so I started taking down my easel.

"I have a gift for you," Gabe told her. "Just wait a little bit, okay?"

"What gift?"

"A big one. Can't tell you yet."

"A big one? Is that a dick joke?"

"No, that would be a fact. This is a real surprise."

"Tell me or you're not getting any for a month."

"I beg to differ," he said, all smiles.

Great, now they were talking about having sex. And here I was so in love with her I'd settled for some of her spit on my cheek like a complete creepy loser. At that moment I'd never envied anyone so much as I envied Gabe. I started packing up even faster, kicked the empty beer cans into a small bush.

"Roger, what's this all—"

"Trust him," I said without looking up. It sounded angry, because I was. Angry that she was with him. Angry that I'd never have her. Angry that I'd never have anyone. Angry that she was being stubborn. All of it triggered flashbacks of killing Skinny Man. Like rapid-fire-bullet memories I saw him again, coming at me with the ax. Me throwing the gun. Him trying to pick it up. Me hacking that

6666666666666666

ax blade into his face. I could smell his hot blood spitting up into my eyes as we fell down together.

"Roger? You okay?" Victoria's voice.

I threw my paintbrushes and paints back in my art tool box and started walking back to my car. As I reached the door she tapped me on the shoulder. I spun around and dropped everything to the ground. "What!"

She stepped back, her mouth agape. We stood staring at each other for a second, then I bent down and started picking up my things.

"Sorry," she said. "It's just . . . you were mumbling something and it sounded—"

"Angry?"

"Yeah." She bent down and helped me pick up the brushes. "Did I do something? Did Gabe do something? I don't know why he made you take a picture. I mean, it's your camera. You didn't have to—"

"It's not that. I'm sorry, really. It has nothing to do with you guys. I just . . . remembered that I have some work to do at home and with Barry needing these paintings I . . . I just realized I'm going to be up all night, is all. Sorry. Didn't mean to get weird and snap at you. I'm really sorry."

We both stood up. She smiled, accepting my apology. That's how she was. Always finding the good in people. Gabe was walking over now. "You okay, Lo Pan?" he asked.

"Yeah. Fine, Mr. Burton," I said.

"Ah! You got that one. Good. Love that movie."

Victoria groaned. "You two should marry each other."

Gabe and I exchanged glances. "Look," I said to Victoria, "stay here and hear what Gabe has to say. I'll swing by the gallery and talk to Barry and tell him you got hung up. Like I said, if he docks your pay I'll cover it. And that's an order, soldier." I added the last part to lighten the mood.

She looked at Gabe, back to me. I think she was starting to catch on now. A big smile spread across her face and she squinted her eyes like she was suddenly privy to a big secret. "Okaaaay." With that, she nodded at me, and I nodded back. We didn't need to say anything else.

I watched them walk back down the small dirt path to the clearing near the water.

Across the lake, lovers still rested on blankets. I wanted to cry. It's not easy to lose something you've spent so long dreaming about. And I don't even mean Victoria—I just mean the idea of having someone to share my life with.

All I have is Skinny Man living in the back of my mind.

Over the next several minutes I loaded up the car, doing my best to hide my disappointment. Gabe took Victoria by the hand and led her off to whatever spot he'd found to pop the question. I debated going back and picking up the beer cans, but I didn't really care about littering any more. Call it my little protest to this whole sad situation, but if I was gonna be bumped out, then so could the Earth. Sue me.

"You'd better take good care of her, Mr. Burton," I said, and then threw the Camaro in gear and sped out of there the way Tooth used to tear donuts on people's lawns. Man, I just wanted another beer and a sleeping pill. Nightmares or not, I wanted this day to be over.

The road back into the city was bumper to bumper as usual, made worse by the setting sun, which came blindingly through the window as if I were under interrogation from God. Who knows, maybe I was? Maybe He was sick of my mood. I knew I was.

God is something that still bugs me. I'm sure it's obvious at this point that not a day goes by that I don't think about what Skinny Man did to Tooth and Jamie, and what part He, God, played in it. Dr. Marsh said it's common for trauma victims to question their belief in God. The more I think about it though, I don't know if we're questioning His existence or motives so much as we feel betrayed and want Him to know it.

The kicker is that I keep a crucifix in the glove compartment. It's on a necklace my mom gave me when I left for California. Not a St. Christopher pendant, patron saint of travel, which most people keep in their car, but Jesus on the cross. Funny how she can still believe in God after her daughter was horribly butchered by a sick maniac with an ax.

God. Makes ya think. If He does exist, and I ever meet Him, we're gonna have a little talk because He's got some explaining to do.

The driver in front of me hit his brakes and stopped short. It was all I could do not to rear end him by swerving into the lane to my left, narrowly missing the car that was passing there.

"Fuck!"

I pulled up next to the guy who'd stopped short and yelled out the window to him. "Fucking pay attention, dick!"

He was a big guy, bushy mustache, neck thicker than a tree stump. "Wanna solve it right now?" He asked it rather politely, like he knew he'd kick my ass.

For a brief moment I seriously considered just getting out and doing it. My anger and depression was so fierce right then I didn't care about dying; I just wanted to kill this guy.

I said nothing and drove past as fast as traffic would allow, which was still at a snail's pace. In the mirror, I caught sight of my face. Twisted, pissed, lost, sad. Fucked. Not for the first time in my life I thought of Batman. Is this how he was able to become who he was? Harness his rage? Use it?

No. Batman wasn't mad, he simply made peace with his anger, accepted it. Then he used it. Two different things, I knew. Me, I was just angry.

You shoulda just killed him, you pussy.

The voice came from the back of my mind. I glanced in the rearview mirror again and saw Skinny Man sitting in the backseat. He held a pair of pliers. He purposefully made the sun glint off them to blind me.

"Medication," I said out loud. Giving myself therapy. "Just get home and take your meds again."

Skinny Man clicked the pliers together. *Meds won't bring them back. Shit, boy, it won't even bring me back. Might as well have slit that guy in that car. Mess him up good. Maybe he's got a sister you can rape with his trachea. I done that once—*

"Shut UP! SHUT THE FUCK UP!" I squinted my eyes, shook my head. Dr. Marsh told me sometimes it helps to count to ten, so I did that. It didn't really work so I thought about a two-headed camel fucking a rocking chair and that finally got my mind off things. I checked the mirror again and sure enough he was gone. Only face I saw there was my own. "Just stress."

I knew it was true—stress can bring on these episodes. Aside from watching the girl I liked just walk off to deal with a marriage proposal—and it was obvious she'd say yes—I still had a lot to do before I could go to bed. I needed to swing by the gallery. I needed to paint that other pic—

"Ah crap." Just like that I realized I hadn't snapped the other photo I needed. I slammed my fists on the steering wheel but caught myself and took a few deep breaths. Last thing I needed were my demons appearing behind me again.

A quick mental calculation of my surroundings did not make the situation any better. I was in between two strip malls—one on the north side of the freeway and one on the south side—and both were bookended by residential neighborhoods. Had there been a small park of some kind nearby I'd have just pulled over and snapped a picture of some trees. But the thing is, remember, the people who buy plein air like to visit the spot. So I couldn't very likely take a picture of a tree that might be in some guy's backyard. Well, I could, and it would be funny, and if Tooth were here he'd call me a wimp for not doing it . . . but I do need to keep my clientele.

Twenty minutes had passed since I'd left the lake, but I was still closer to that location than anything else worth painting. The sun was dropping, but if I took the next exit and weaved around slow cars, I could still have enough light to jump out and snap a pic.

"Just fucking great." I managed to get to the far right lane and take the next exit. Cars were backed up at the light, so it took a good seven or eight minutes to flip across the bridge and get back on the freeway going east again.

Chapter 6

It took about twenty-five minutes to get back to the lake. Victoria's car was still parked in the dirt lot. Chances were they were making out under a tree somewhere. I loathed the thought she might see me and come over to tell me the news. I'd probably just nod.

I grabbed the camera and walked to the spot where'd I'd been painting. I needed something a bit different than before—people don't want identical paintings. Finally, I settled on taking one from the other side of the lake.

As I made my way across the dirt and weeds I kept my eye out for Victoria, but didn't see her anywhere. Perhaps they'd snuck off to do something more than make out? I walked along the water's edge for a minute and then turned around and snapped a couple of pictures of the trees near the picnic tables. *Good enough*, I thought, and started back to the car. Barry was sure to flip out something fierce at this rate.

When I got back to the lot, I threw the camera in the car, got in, and scanned the horizon. Still didn't see Gabe and Victoria anywhere. "She's gone, idiot, just let it go."

I started the car and began to pull out but stopped quick.

Gabe's cigarette pack was on the ground near Victoria's car. The pack was open and I could see a good ten or twelve smokes in there. I turned the car off and got out.

I would have just assumed he'd dropped them, was just gonna put them on the car's hood for him, but when I got out and picked up the pack, something else struck me.

There was blood on it. I squatted down and looked at the dirt where the pack had been. More blood.

Something inside me felt wrong. I was suddenly experiencing some innate sense of alertness. A shitload of scenarios ran through my mind: the ring had gotten stuck and they'd had to yank it off and cut her finger, or maybe one of them had just tripped and opened a gash on their knee or something. Neither explained why the car was still here.

I checked the doors to be safe. They were locked. Now, for the first time, I saw what looked like a handprint on the back window. A bloody handprint.

"The fuck?" I said, taking out my cell phone. I dialed Victoria and let it ring until her voicemail picked up. "Hey, it's me. Roger. Just making sure you're okay. I had to come back for something and found Gabe's smokes and . . . well, there's some blood and . . . anyway, gimme a call."

I hung up and waited about two minutes but she never called back.

I took one of Gabe's cigarettes and lit it with my car lighter. When I was done smoking it, staring at my phone and the lake, I tried her number again. Still no answer.

Now my spider sense was *really* tingling.

Then I noticed that the SUV wasn't parked on the other side of the lake anymore. It hadn't passed by me since I got back, although it could have just gone out the back road.

"Fuck it." I dialed 911. It rang and rang, then told me if I had an emergency I should stay on the line. I'd called 911 once before since moving to California, to report a car bumper in the middle of the freeway. They hadn't answered then either. Taxpayer dollars at work.

I hung up and dialed Teddy. He answered quickly, probably had my number programmed in. "Roger? What's up? Those idiots at the website—"

"No. I . . . um . . . I think maybe my friends are in trouble." As I say this I'm getting strobing images from those days in Skinny Man's cellar. I can hear that ax hacking up Jamie in the back room and I'm trying real hard not to lose it.

"What do you mean?" He sounded tired. It was close to 9:30 P.M. on the east coast and I knew he worked long days so he was probably in bed.

I told him about the bloody cigarette pack and handprint. I told him about the guys in the SUV who'd been staring us down earlier. We lingered in silence for a few seconds. Then: "Roger, it could be anything."

"I know. That's what scares me."

"You call the police?"

"911 is busy. The song is true. Long live Flavor Flav."

"Okay, I'm gonna see if I can get through to anyone there. You stay put in case they come back. Don't worry, they're probably just walking around somewhere."

"And the blood?"

"Yeah. I know. I'm just trying to sound positive. But I'm serious, don't do anything 'til you hear from me."

We hung up.

I got in my car and drove around to the other side of the lake, parked where the SUV had been. Other people were getting in their cars and leaving. I checked the ground and saw a number of different dirt tire tracks leading out, most heading back toward the avocado stand, but some taking the back way as well. One of them might have been the SUV. But shit, it's not like I knew the difference between SUV tread and a frigging Big Wheel.

The nearby weeds revealed nothing, no clues, no tell tales signs that something might have happened. Just some bugs that hightailed it at my approach.

The guy with the dog was packing up his things and putting them in his car.

I waved to him. "Hey."

He looked at me, kind of suspicious. "Howdy."

"Looking for my friends. Guy and a girl. She has glasses, really cute. He's got a black T-shirt and tattoos. You seen them?"

He nodded. Pointed off to my left. "Earlier. They were walking up on that small hill there."

Must be where Gabe proposed.

"There was a white SUV here. You see it leave?"

His suspicious look intensified. "Yeah, it left a little while ago."

"Which way?"

He pointed out toward the back road. The way he turned and left made it clear he wanted nothing more to do with me. I said thanks anyway and made my way up the hill he'd seen Gabe and Victoria on. It was empty now. Some of the grass looked flattened. Yeah, I'm a regular Sherlock Holmes.

My cell phone rang. It was Teddy. "Roger, I spoke to a detective out there but there's nothing he can do. It's not a missing person's report until twenty-four hours."

"Are you fucking serious? We haven't overruled that bullshit timeframe? Teddy, there's a full-on bloody handprint on the car. Trust me on this one, something is up. You for one should know that bad shit happens in a matter of minutes."

"I know, but I'm in New Hampshire, three thousand miles away. The cops there don't know you and if they did they'd just think you were freaking out based on your past."

"C'mon! Okay, so what? I sit tight and see if they come back?"

"Or call and report something suspicious, at least to get a cruiser out there. Talk to whoever shows up, but I can't guarantee it'll come to anything yet. Show them the blood. Give me your friend's license plate number."

"Okay. Hang on." I walked over to the car and read it to him. I also took a picture of the bloody handprint with my cell phone and sent it to his email for whatever good it would do.

I could hear him booting up his home computer on the other end. "Okay. I'll get her DMV photo from the database and see if I can't get anyone else out there to look at it. The handprint might help, it might not."

"Thanks, Teddy. Now give me some advice: if it was you, and your friends disappeared, and you found fresh blood on their car—"

"I'd go with my gut. Try to think like a perp and see what made sense. If it felt wrong, I'd call in my officers and get everyone out there."

"And the SUV?"

"Well, if you believe it has something to do with this—"

"They were definitely punchy-looking guys. Looked at us like they wanted to stomp us out."

"Ok. Well, I'd see if I could figure out which way it went."

"Already did, but a lot of cars go that way. Can you spot SUV treads?"

"Sometimes. They're bigger and wider. A lot them are non-directional—"

"Meaning what?"

"Meaning the split in the middle of the tread will actually be off-center. The tires get rotated from the front axle to the back, but never from one side of the vehicle to the other, like you do with Sedans. But honestly, the odds—"

"Ok, thanks. I'll figure it out."

"Wait, Roger, don't do anything dumb. Call the cops like I said and just give a bullshit report to get them out there. I'll be in touch, okay?"

We hung up. I was back at my car in seconds, bending over to study the various treads in the dirt lot. There were a shit load of them. Most were scuffed or only half visible. They all went the same route so what was I really hoping I'd find?

There. Treads with an off-center split. Okay, so Teddy knew a lot about tires. Had to give him that. The tread led out to the back road, just like the guy with the dog had said. So far so good.

I took Teddy's advice and called the cops again, and this time they answered. I made up a story. "Hi, yeah, there's some guys fighting out here at Corazon Del Agua. You should really send some cars."

The dispatcher told me she'd get the nearest car in the area to respond, then hung up.

I waited another five minutes, my pulse getting faster with each ticking second. No cops arrived. Finally, I said screw it and drove out to the back road. The dirt lot gave over to asphalt. Different tire treads went left and right. I hopped out and bent down like some kind of wannabe forensic investigator, tried to make out treads from an SUV.

"This is ridiculous."

Nothing.

Back in the car, I sat staring out the windshield. The sky was deep pink now, maybe a half hour from complete sunset. Maybe less.

I'd go with my gut.

Taking a right would start me back toward civilization. Would they have gone back to a populated area?

Try to think like a perp . . .

Taking a left would put me out near the casino, into the desert. It was secluded, but that was the problem—nowhere to really go.

If it felt wrong . . .

It all felt wrong, and way too familiar.
. . . I'd call in my officers and get everyone out there.
It was just me out here.
I went left.

Chapter 7

Nothing existed out in the direction I decided to head. I saw a couple of signs with mileage countdowns to the casino (30 miles, 25 miles, 20 miles . . .) but as far as the surrounding landscape was concerned, it was nothing but stretches of dirt, and the occasional cactus plant or sere shrubs. This was what they called "inland" in Southern California, a term that was generally spit out like an epithet. You didn't venture inland unless you had given up on life, were headed to a casino, or had acquired some rustic, eroding property through a death in the family.

I scanned the barren land around me as I drove, hoping for signs of something, anything, that might give insight into this strange situation. Just looked like a lot of empty earth to me.

Of course rational thought tried to sway me the entire time. *Maybe nothing happened. Maybe Gabe and Victoria were fucking in the bushes and didn't want to be found. Maybe what you thought was blood was just strawberry juice.*

"Maybe you should shut the hell up and let me drive."

The sky was deep purple now, practically night. The hills became the shadowy humps of a giant beast undulating across the land; I was a mite running across its hide, driven by a need to feast on clarification. I had to know where they'd gone.

The minutes passed in silence; I'd left the iPod off so I could think, but it wasn't really amounting to much. I really wanted a cigarette.

Gabe's pack was still in my pocket so I took it out and lit up another one. Truth be told, I wasn't a smoker, but there's something to be said for the calming placebo effect of a good smoke. Call it sad justification if you want, it calmed my nerves.

I rolled down the driver's side window to let the smoke out, let the night air in—a peaceful trade. It was getting chilly outside, but the cool breeze helped keep me focused.

"Where are you bastards?"

No answer. Only a few cars passed me going the other way—a bit odd for what I thought was a heavily-trafficked casino back route—after which I was mostly alone save for a pair of taillights up ahead. Could it be them? I doubted it. Still, I had to know so I sped up and got close. It was a beat up Hyundi something or other. I flashed on my highbeams and made out the silhouette of a woman driving. She flicked her mirror down to redirect the glare of my beams and flipped me off through the back window. Fair enough, I thought, and eased up off her ass.

"C'mon, c'mon." My urgent pleas for help drifted out the window with the smoke. "Just give me something. Where the hell would they go? The casino? What, are they all playing craps?"

I pitched the spent cigarette out the window as I passed by a rocky ridge and my hat came off in the sudden wind. It whipped up, struck the ceiling of the car, and danced out the window.

"You gotta be kidding me!"

I hit the brakes and flipped a U-turn. Thankfully, I found it on the side of the road a few yards back, a little worse for wear. Not like the damn thing hadn't seen enough hard times as it was. But it's a sentimental article and I wasn't about to let it go.

I pulled over into the berm and kept my lights on it, got out and reached down for it. And shuddered.

It was resting on tire tracks. Non-directional tread etched into the ground. The same from the lake.

"Well I'll be a two-headed camel in Ikea."

I bent down and got a closer look at the tracks, ran my hand over them. The dirt wasn't hard or dry and it crumbled under my touch. Whether that categorized it as "fresh" I couldn't tell you. But it certainly wasn't old.

The tracks turned off the road, out across the barren land, toward some lights on the near horizon that looked like a town. Whoever had driven off the road here felt like taking a shortcut.

"In a hurry?"

Stop talking to yourself, faggot boy.

The voice was Skinny Man's but I did my best to ignore it. That was enough—I wanted to get back on my meds.

I got back in the car and pulled off into the dirt. The car bounced up and down along the dusty ground like the tits of a jumping, braless fat lady. A couple of times I swept into a pothole of sorts and heard the car's undercarriage wail in protest. Forget it, I was on a mission. If I busted it, so what? I'd seen Camaros in worse shape, that was for sure.

The lights drew closer and I could see it wasn't really a town, but a couple of ranches. People out this way had horses, I knew, and I wondered if I'd ride through an electric fence and fry myself. Zoning laws are weird in rural areas; I know, I grew up in one. I also faced death in one because of those same stupid laws.

It looked like three ranches spread out on a small road. Lights burned in the windows of all. Other lights had been tacked to posts or gates around the properties, probably so they could lead their animals around at night. Or have keg parties. Whichever.

Another couple of minutes and I was across the open dirt and moving into the property line of the house directly ahead of me. No fence. That was good. I killed the headlights and drove by moonlight, easing my way toward what looked like a driveway. A small barn stood off to my left, and to my right, a chicken coop. Great, that's all I needed, some annoying birds alerting Tombstone that Billy the Kid had come to play cowboy.

The birds, thankfully, didn't give two shits about cars in their yard. Or maybe they were used to them. Maybe the owners owned dirt bikes or something and noise was a norm for them. Anyway, they didn't squawk.

The driveway turned out to be paved and had a basketball net and what looked like a street hockey net at its tip. Some BMX bikes were lying on their side next to a Ford F-150 and a dirty Ford Focus. Take note, kids, Inlanders like to Fix Or Repair Daily.

I skirted wide of the vehicles and brought myself out onto the road in front of the small ranch house, parked along the side. The sound of some horse whinnies meandered through the night. Figured the barn was actually a stable. Beyond that, I heard nothing but night sounds—crickets, some eucalyptus trees rustling, the very faint swoosh of cars on a main road somewhere nearby. Must be pretty close to the casino I gathered. It was dinnertime for most, but gambling habits knew nothing of time or distance.

The sky was really black out here, loaded with stars, as if some-one had hung black velvet in front of a light and then unloaded buckshot into it. I tried to remember what I knew of astronomy, which came mostly from cheap science fiction novels, but all I really made out was Orion's Belt and the Big Dipper. I hadn't seen so many stars since New Hampshire. The whole scene had weight: the clear night sky, the lonely ranches, the horses chuffing somewhere close. Kind of felt romantic. It made me think about Victoria. About the bloody handprint on her car.

I took my keys out of the ignition, planning on opening my trunk with them, but never got that far.

There was a man looking in my back window. He banged his hand on my trunk. "The fuck you doing!"

Shit, was this one of the guys I'd seen at the lake? Would he remember me? On the floor of my back seat was my steering wheel club. As slowly as I could, I reached back and brought it up into my lap. Then I opened the door and leaned out, keeping my weapon hidden. "Lost," I replied. "You know where I am?"

He walked towards me, came around the driver's side. My hand squeezed the club tighter as I shut the door again.

"Yer on my fucking property. I just seen you drive across my fucking yard! What the fuck was that shit? You fucking drunk or something. Fuck!"

This guy really needed to have Santa bring him a thesaurus.

"Sorry about that. I saw a car do it earlier so I thought maybe it was some kinda road."

"Road? Are you kidding me? Get outta that car." He reached for the door handle.

"Don't." I hit the lock and had one of my moments again, the kind where I have to test myself. The kind where I looked him right in the eye and dared him to open the door. He hesitated, kinda looked back at me. He was big, rustic, missing a tooth, a cliché from a trucker movie, the kind of simpleton goon that would tear a person my size to shreds. But I'm willing to bet he'd never seen some-one my size look at him like that before.

Yeah, that's right, Bubba, it ain't the size of the dog in the fight. I've known pain before, worse than you, and I'm not afraid.

The window was open but at least now if he wanted me he'd

have to reach inside . . . where I had my club. "I'm not looking for a fight," I added. "I'm real sorry I drove across your yard. Like I said, I saw someone else—"

"Who? Tell me and I'll shoot the fucker in the face."

I decided to risk mentioning the SUV. If this was one of the guys, his reaction might give him away, if not, then maybe he knew who the SUV belonged to. "White Pathfinder, maybe a Bronco, couldn't really tell."

"Nothing like that here." He seemed sincere.

"Maybe one of the neighbors?"

He scratched his head like I'd stumped him with too many questions at once. "Not that I know of. Not with a white girlie car like that. Don't talk to them much so . . . oh wait, guy lives up the hill there a bit. I think I seen him with a white piece of shit like you saying. I don't know the fucker's name but he's on my shit list now. You see him you tell him Leslie's coming for him."

Leslie? Well that explained his violent tendencies. That must have been hell to go through school with that name . . . if in fact he'd even gone to school.

I tipped my hat to him. "I will. Thanks for understanding. You . . . uh . . . have a nice home."

He arched his back and rubbed his big beer belly. "Meh, it ain't much but it's mine. Well, mine and my wife's. She wanted horses and I wanted a place where people wouldn't bug me. Kids bug the shit outta me though. You see them? Out there?" He pointed out toward the dark stretch of desert. "They ran out to play ten minutes ago and I can't find 'em and *American Idol* starts in, like, five minutes and I am not missing that on account of these shits out there with their B.B. guns trying to shoot coyotes." He pronounced it Kai-Oats. "I need to vote for that Kentucky kid, what's his name . . . Trevor Booth. You hear him sing?"

"No. I don't watch the show."

"Shit, son, you missing out. Wait. What was I asking you?"

"If I'd seen your kids."

He burped. Then: "Right. The kids. You didn't see 'em?"

"No. Didn't see anyone."

"Well, you do, you fucking run 'em over and tell 'em I want 'em home."

Apparently he'd forgotten all about kicking my ass.

"Will do." I pointed up the road, up a small hill. "You say the guy with the white truck lives up there?"

"Think so. Why?" He looked at me suspiciously, like I'd been lying to him about something.

"Figured I'd drive by and see if it was the same SUV. If it is I'll come back and let you know. Put a note on your car or something."

He broke into a shit-eating grin. "You do that. You do just that, son. That fucker ain't gonna know what hit him."

Yeah right, soon as *American Idol* starts you'll probably forget we even talked.

I said bye and drove off up the hill. It was dark and I didn't want to put the lights on to reveal my presence just yet. I kept asking myself if this was all crazy. What if I got there, saw the truck, knocked on their door and they were just some normal rednecks? I'd have wasted my time and proved nothing.

The house in question was about a half mile from Leslie's place. Far enough away to not know your neighbor, but I wouldn't say it was secluded; through the eucalyptus trees along the road I could still see the lights on Leslie's barn. The place had its own garage but I couldn't see inside it. There was only one way to know for sure.

I parked on the road, got out and made my way up the driveway, hoping a motion detector light wouldn't snap on. Nothing gave me away. There was one window on the side of the garage that I pressed my face up against. Some boxes had been stacked in front of it on the inside but I was pretty sure there was a car in there, and it looked white.

From somewhere in the house there was a loud crash.

Someone screamed.

A woman.

Chapter 8

I braced myself for a woman to come running out with an ax in her head, braced myself for a tattooed man with death in his eyes to run out after her, but instead everything went silent. My muscles tightened into ropes, my fists balled, my ears searched for other sounds of distress.

The lack of any further nefarious noises sang in my head. A big silent alarm. What the fuck was that scream?

A short sprint brought me around to the back of the house. Like Leslie's little ranch, this one also had an open dirt backyard that stretched off toward the hills. No chickens or horses here, though. No lawn furniture, no basketball nets, no signs of life. The house was a one-story stucco deal with a red clay roof—pretty much the same as every other house in Southern California. You know the stuff. If you've seen one you've seen them all. Carbon-copied society, just add water. Someone had hung black drapes inside all of the windows so it was hard to see anything inside.

Pressing my ear against the side of the house, I could make out faint voices from within. Someone was grunting, someone was laughing, someone was crying. For all I knew they were watching a movie or playing a board game. Still, it felt odd.

Then, from inside, there came another desperate scream. Except this time it was muffled, like someone screaming into a pillow.

The black drapes in front of me fluttered as someone rushed by them. Another person charged by right after. Stampeding feet shook the house.

Someone yelled, "Git back here!"

I had just enough time to see a guy in blue jeans and a wifebeater tackle someone in a black T-shirt into a refrigerator before they spun to the ground. Wrestling. Punching. Biting. The fridge door opened and spilled condiments and beer bottles into the melee. The walls of the house vibrated in time with the fight as fists and feet flew.

The drapes fell back in place but left a crack of visibility for me. I felt a chill watching the two people wrestling on the ground. The sounds of knuckles smashing into flesh smacked through the air. And even though I could only make out part of the scene—a wild snapshot of cartwheeling legs—it was obvious this was a real fight. Not two friends goofing around. There was going to be blood involved. Bones were going to break and muscles would tear. But then Wifebeater got an advantage, punched his nemesis in the face, and knocked him out cold.

"Got 'im," he yelled. "Ow. Motherfucker. Hurt my hand."

From another room: "Tie 'em up good this time, you retard."

A third voice joined in from somewhere else as well: "Hurry up, I'm almost done!"

Wifebeater picked up his catch under the arms and began dragging the guy across the floor. Just before they disappeared through an archway, I saw the unconscious man's face.

Gabe.

My stomach dropped out from under me and my knees went weak. It was happening again. The violence, the pain. Random acts of hatred by a sick world.

The muffled screaming, still playing in the background somewhere, became agonizing sobs of pain and terror. Someone was grunting, something was banging against something else, a repetitious slapping filled with human shame. I knew exactly what it sounded like.

I knew what they were doing to Victoria.

"I'm next," someone declared. "Hurry up. I want her ass. Don't mess that up for me. I want it tight!"

Bile rose in my throat. It was all I could do to keep breathing.

"Almost . . . nhhh . . . done. Oh man, I'm gonna cum. Yeah! Wake that kid up, I want him to watch. I want him to see me fill his bitch's mouth."

"Wake up, punk. Come on, your girlie's about to take it on the chin, no pun intended."

All three men were laughing now, one of them between grunts. It was a party to them, a cheap thrill at the expense of a human being.

"He's awake now. He's awake. Hey, boy! Hey, watch this! I'm gonna CUM!"

Victoria cried. The type of cry I'd never heard before, not even in Skinny Man's basement. If I'd been present at Jesus' crucifixion, I imagine his followers would have cried this way. A complete loss of faith in anything good, a complete acceptance of the absolute horror that rules the Earth.

Gabe said something but I couldn't make it out because it was mostly a howling cry of horror, hatred and shame.

I closed my eyes and saw Skinny Man. He was laughing, waving at me. The world around him was raining blood and he was curling his finger at me in a come hither gesture.

Walk back into your world of death, Roger. You belong here. Just break the window and jump inside. Rule your world as only you know how. Show them how you deal with bad people. Show them your gift for drawing blood. No. Not. Yet.

I opened my eyes.

My gun was in my trunk. I needed to get it now and call the cops. But I couldn't move. Not out of fear, but out of indecision. I *did* want to break the window and throw myself inside, but I doubted I could take all three guys by myself; if I went for my gun, it might be enough time for them to kill Victoria.

From inside: "Done. She's all yours."

"What the hell, man, I thought you were gonna do it on her face. It's all leaking out across her asshole now. I don't want to fuck your jizz."

"Quit complaining, you fucking homo. What's it matter if you're just gonna fuck her shitter anyway. Just flip her over and do her that way. Hurry up, Bob's up next. And hey, missy, quit crying. You know you like it. C'mon, wipe those tears away."

There was a smack that echoed throughout the house. Victoria went silent for a second, then yelped. Then cried again. Gabe was out of his mind, a blathering stooge forced to watch his one true love ripped to pieces and destroyed forever.

I made up my mind. Gun. Now.

I took one step back the way I'd come when my phone rang.

"Shit," I whispered. I plucked the phone from my back pocket and flipped it open. It was Teddy.

"What was that?" It was one of the rapists inside. "I heard something outside. Bob, go check it out. Now!"

I spoke quickly as I raced back toward the driveway: "Teddy, trace my cell."

"What? Roger, you okay?"

I rounded the garage. Passed the window with the boxes stacked inside. My car in sight at the end of the drive.

"Teddy, just trace—"

He came out of nowhere, a big burly man with a wiry beard and long, greasy hair. I just had enough time to make out the Budweiser T-shirt he wore before I saw the shovel coming right at me. It swung into my face with the force of a fucking Cruz missile. Stars exploded behind my eyes. The bones in my face shifted, cracked, slid around under my skin. I felt the shock all the way down to my feet. The pain was too intense to even scream. I merely fought to breathe, to stay conscious. The excruciating fire in my skull then jumped a level as my nerves registered everything they were feeling and I was suddenly falling, hitting cement, lying flat on my back and twitching. Thick blood gushed down my throat, threatening to suffocate me, dribbling down across my cheeks and dripping off my earlobes to the ground.

My eyes wouldn't open, or maybe I was just dead, seeing the blackness of a disappointing afterlife. I sure as shit felt dead.

"Gotcha, you dumb motherfucker." It was Mr. Budweiser, Mr. Grand Slam Hitter, standing above me. He called back to his friends. "I got 'im. That kid from the park. The one they were with."

A voice in the darkness: "Bring him in here."

The phone was still in my hand and faintly I could hear Teddy calling my name. Didn't matter though, I couldn't move, couldn't think, couldn't do anything but fight the insane pressure building up in my face. Couldn't even moan.

Mr. Budweiser grabbed my arm and began to drag me, and again I felt my face slide across an infinite field of agony. That's when I realized my nose was broken. Mashed into a thousand shards of bone.

My body was hauled up some small steps and into the house, and yanked through a couple of rooms I couldn't make out because my eyes were now swelling up. Maybe I saw a refrigerator, some beer cans, a light above me. Not sure.

Then, into the room with Victoria and Gabe. I could hear them now—Victoria crying through a gag, Gabe sobbing and shaking somewhere to my right. I was dropped on the ground in the middle of the room.

"Take his phone."

Someone grabbed my cell phone and spoke into it: "He'll call you back." Then it was thrown to the ground in front of me. What looked like a boot came down and crushed it.

"Holy shit. What the fuck did you hit him with?"

"Shovel."

"Fuckin-A, he looks like roadkill. Hey, Bob, hurry up and finish with that bitch. We have a new problem to take care of."

I forced my eyes open despite the pain it caused. Through narrow slits I could make out the scene more clearly: Victoria was bent over a weight bench, her arms tied to the barbell rests with some nylon cord. A large man was behind her, thrusting forward with enough velocity to break through a concrete wall. Gabe was next to them, tied to a chair. His face was bloody and his shirt was torn. Wide-eyed, he watched the horror show in front of him.

A third man stood over me as well, but from the floor I couldn't see his face.

With a primal grunt Bob finished what he was doing and pulled himself out of Victoria. He moved aside as he zipped up his pants and I could see Victoria's naked bottom. Her pants had been ripped off and her ass was beet red. I saw everything between her legs, and what they'd done to it in their fits of power. A day ago I'd have given anything to see Victoria naked. But not like this. Not with the blood and semen and bruises. She was no longer a human being, they'd taken that from her. She was just a piece of used up meat now, sagging slowly off the weight bench.

I looked away.

I tried to tell them what I was going to do to them. "Kill you," I muttered.

Mr. Budweiser leaned down in front of me. "What's that?"

"Kill you."

"Oh, I think not, pussyboy." He kicked me in the gut and I went fetal. My insides felt like they were swelling up inside of me.

Bob slicked his messed-up hair back, flicked open a jackknife and cut Victoria's binds. She finally fell all the way to the ground in front of me. Our eyes met, but she was not seeing me. Just staring through me. Unlike myself and Gabe, these rapists had not messed up her face. It was red from enduring her torture, and slick with tears and running mascara, but her beauty was unmistakable—angelic features, adorable small nose, intense green eyes. I died a bit right there. All over again. Just like ten years ago when I watched Tooth go; like when I found Jamie. Ten years of rebuilding my sense of humanity gone in a flash. I felt nothing but hatred. Sheer, focused hatred of a type that wraps around you like a shield. I welcomed this hatred, because it was something I knew very well. It was my old friend come back to say hi.

That's right, Roger, use that hatred. Spill their blood all over the place.

In his chair, Gabe began to shout furiously, shocking me out of my daze.

"No! No! Victoria!"

"Shut him up," Mr. Budweiser said. Bob, who I now saw was bald and had a tattoo of an eagle on his scalp, punched Gabe in the ear. Gabe's head slammed into his own shoulder and he went silent, but he never once took his eyes off his fiancée.

The third man, the largest of the three, knelt down in front of me. Like Mr. Budweiser he had a big beard and a tattoo of a sparrow on his neck. He wore a big jean jacket with biker patches on them. A crucifix hung around his neck next to an Iron Cross. "Who'd you call?"

I said nothing.

"You call the cops? Answer me." He grabbed my nose and squeezed. White-hot electricity coursed through my entire body. Now, for the first time, I screamed. There are some pains you can't fight.

"Shut up! Shut up! You don't and I squeeze even harder, got me?"

With effort, I stopped screaming and he let go of my nose.

"You called the cops, didn't you?"

"Kill you."

"Yeah yeah, I heard that one already."

Mr. Budweiser grabbed my hair. "What'd you tell them? Are

they on the way? Did you even get to speak to anyone?"

"Kill you."

"Dipshit, you're not going to kill anyone. But depending on what you tell me, I may or may not put the bullet in your head as opposed to your stomach. Get me? Now, who did you speak to?"

I decided to bluff them. "Cops. On the way here now. Ten seconds or so."

Mr. Budweiser picked up the broken phone. "He's lying. The number on it wasn't a local area code. Wasn't 911 neither. I don't think it was the cops."

Bob stepped forward. "Shit, Walt, we gotta get outta here. What if it was, like, the FBI or something. Don't they do kidnappings?"

Walt, the guy with the sparrow on his neck, stood up and snatched Bob by the throat, pulled him close. "Use my name again and I'll put a bullet in *your* head. Second, we can't leave yet. We gotta clean her up first." He pointed down to Victoria.

"We don't have time." Bob looked to Mr. Budweiser for help. Clearly Mr. Budweiser knew better than to cross Walt because he just shrugged. Bob forged on by himself. "We gotta get outta here and burn this place. I ain't going back to the joint, man. I like real pussy too much. I like real steak, too. We need to go."

Walt shook his head. "Not yet. Goldilocks specifically said not to touch the girl. Remember? And we did. Our gunk is all over her. So we got to clean her first."

Bob pointed to Gabe. "So just say she was fucking that douchebag when we found them. Let's go."

"Listen, you dumb mongoloid, they won't buy that. We drop her off in this condition they'll know we had fun with her and that'll be the end of us. This is a good gig and I ain't losing it because you're hasty. So we need to fix her up *first*." He finally let go of Bob and knelt down in front of me again. As he spoke he reached over and slid his hand up Victoria's shirt and played with her breasts. She began to shake and whimper. "Besides, couldn't have been calling the cops anyway. It was *his* phone that rang. My guess is" —he played his hand around my nose, now speaking to me—"you got a call from a friend. That's it, isn't it? Not cops. Just some lame friend. But did you tell this friend where you were is the question?"

"Yes."

"You're lying. I can see it in your black eyes." He tapped my nose and the pain flushed across my vision. "Yeah, I know I'm right. Ain't no cops coming."

That settled that. Walt seemed satisfied he had time to kill and went into leader mode. He grabbed Victoria by her ankle and dragged her over to Mr. Budweiser. "Take her in the bathroom and clean her up. Make her look nice. Get all the shit outta her ass and stuff."

"What? Didn't say nothing about giving her an enema before!"

"Not an enema, you inbred freakfest, just clean all of the jizz outta her. Then wipe that running makeup off her face." He turned to Bob. "You, get this place ready to blaze. Make sure it goes up fast so there's no chance of DNA evidence. Oil rags in every corner. And give me that shovel."

Mr. Budweiser nodded and handed the shovel to Walt. Bob picked up Victoria and made her walk to a bathroom just off of the room we were in. Her legs barely worked and gravity made a mess of pink goo slide down her inner thighs. For the first time I saw the gun in the back of Bob's waistband and I put two and two together and realized they all had guns on them somewhere. No doubt that's how they got Gabe to cooperate.

A second later water ran and Bob made lewd remarks to Victoria as he washed her up. Gabe was trying to look over his shoulder to make sure she was okay but she was out of sight. Hearing her small moans was worse, because it let our imaginations go wild. Was Bob just cleaning her up, or was he doing something else? Was he violating her with his fingers?

Don't dwell on that, I told myself. *You know how that whole thing goes. Just ignore it. Focus on Walt and his two rapist retard minions.*

I scanned the room for weapons, anything the might help in a fight. Only thing I found was the barbell for the weight set. It was leaning up against the far wall but I'd have to rush past Walt to get it. Maybe if I caught him off guard, confused him somehow, I might make it there. It was the only option I had.

Walt approached me, shovel still in his hand, and pulled a gun from the back of his waistband. He bent down and tapped me in the nose with it. Again, my face lit up with heat and pressure.

"Okay, bitch, roll over."

I sneered. "Why, you gonna rape me, too?"

"Nah. Well, maybe with the shovel if you don't shut up. But not right now. Roll over." He jabbed me with the shovel and forced me to turn away from him. I felt his hands going into my back pocket and realized he was pulling out my wallet. When he stood up, he removed my license. Memories of Skinny Man doing the same thing danced in my head. I rolled back over and looked up at him, eyeing the barbell behind him every couple of seconds. He put my wallet in his own back pocket. "Roger. That's a gay name. You must really hate your parents. Giving you a gay name and all."

"Well, they were gonna go with Walt, but they wanted to give me a chance."

"Oh, you're a tough guy. Bet you *would* like this shovel in your ass."

"Seems more like you're just dying to get up in my blowhole. Puts a real smile on your face. So who's the one with the real homosexual issues?"

"Hardy har. Here, smell this." He let the blade of the shovel swing leisurely into my face. Yeah, it hurt, but I was getting real pissed now and it helped me push any hope of surviving out of my head. Sometimes that's better, you know, to know you're going to die. Then you just don't care about the stupidity of fighting back. You just do it.

"I'm not afraid of you, Walt." I could still hear Victoria's moans from the back room.

"You know what?" He pointed the gun at my face. "I don't really care. Get up and stand over there." He indicated the wall behind me with his gun and I followed suit, happy to be on my feet again. As I moved he kept his gun trained on me. Now I was even farther from the barbell.

Mr. Budweiser came back from wherever he'd been, carrying an empty gasoline container. "All set, Walt. Place will flare up in seconds."

Walt nodded. "Good." He yelled over his shoulder: "Bob, get that bitch in the truck. We're gonna get going. Time to get paid."

A second later Bob and Victoria returned. Her face was blank, and I could see she was having difficulty walking. They shuffled past us and out of the room, presumably to the garage.

"What about these two?" Mr. Budweiser looked back and forth at me and Gabe.

Walt scratched his nose with his gun, then hefted his shovel. "You untie the boyfriend. I'll take this other one. We'll do it out back. C'mon. And no funny moves, Roger, or I will follow through on my promise of showing this shovel your intestines first."

Mr. Budweiser took out his own gun and untied Gabe. As soon as the last binding was off Gabe threw a punch. It connected with Mr. Budweiser's chin and dazed him. Here's my chance, I thought, and took a step toward Walt, planning on kicking him in the groin. But that didn't happen; Walt saw my movement and backhanded me with the gun, catching me in the mouth. As I stumbled back, feeling my tongue swell and mouth fill with blood, I saw him bring the shovel around and whack Gabe in the stomach. Gabe doubled over and fought for breath. It was enough time for Mr. Budweiser to get a kick in to Gabe's head for good measure. And that was that. The match was over.

"Hopalong fucking Cassidy, the balls on these two!" Walt yelled. "I am losing my patience. Now everybody get outside or I will put a bullet in that bitch's head."

We walked out through the kitchen, me and Gabe in front, and Walt and his crony behind us with their guns at our backs. We entered the garage through a door off the kitchen and passed by the white SUV. Victoria was inside, looking out the rear side window at us; I couldn't tell if she saw us or not. It was pretty dark in the garage, and she still looked out of her head, in some kind of safe spot in her mind.

Chapter 9

With the exception of some stridulating beetles in the eucalyptus trees, the backyard was quiet. Above our heads the gray rind of a moon fought to get its light through thick cloud cover. In the distance I could make out the halogen halos from streetlamps reflecting off some low fog. All in all it was pretty serene and warm. A nice night for offing two guys behind a house out in the eastern foothills.

"Keep digging, dickheads," Walt said. He stood behind us with his gun trained on our heads. He was wearing my Red Sox cap. Gabe and I exchanged looks as we dug our own graves with the shovel. The unspoken necessity to take out Walt hung between our eyes. He was going to kill us either way, and if we didn't figure out how to get away he and his friends were going to kill Victoria. Or deliver her to someone who would. They'd made it clear they had kidnapped her for someone else. But who and why?

Thinking about it made my already-pounding head feel worse. Gabe grunted in pain, his own head swimming with dizziness as he clawed more dirt out of the ground. In the condition we were in, this was going to take a while.

"Put some backbone into it, Roger."

"What about if you dig, Walt, and we just jump in the hole when you're done?" I shot him a sarcastic smile, but through my swollen eyes I could barely see his response.

"I don't do manual labor."

"Why don't you just shoot us?" Gabe asked.

"Honestly? Because I see this shit in movies all the time. Supposed to be psychologically terrifying to dig your own grave. I wanna see how it makes you feel. I'm all for life experience, you know. Hell, maybe I'll really take a liking to it and start a new hobby."

I tossed another clump of dirt next to the hole we were digging. "Watch my shoes," Walt said. "They're new."

Gabe used his hands, throwing fistfuls of dirt into the air over his head. He was still looking at me, a thousand scenarios of death and escape swirling in his eyes. I frantically thought of a way out, but could think of nothing besides throwing the shovel at Walt and hoping he didn't fire the gun before it hit him. Problem was he was being smart, standing a little ways back so we couldn't get to him before he could get a shot off.

The minutes passed more quickly than I would have liked, and every second that I didn't come up with a plan was a second closer we came to death.

"Okay, you know what . . ." Gabe sat down in the depression we'd made in the ground. "I'm done. I'm not digging anymore. You want me dead, just do it. But you'd better check the shadows every night because I swear to you I will come back and haunt—"

BANG!

The bright flash of the muzzle caught me off guard. I felt the bullet whiz by my head and heard it punch through something hard. Wetness struck the back of my neck. Trembling, I stopped digging and turned around. Gabe sat still, his eyes open and staring back at me, a giant red hole in the center of his throat. Then, slowly, blood gushed out and he fell forward, his hands reaching to the bullet wound. He tried desperately to keep breathing, the sound like someone walking through mud.

I dropped the shovel and grabbed him. "Gabe! Hang on."

He was shaking, blood gushing out everywhere. "No. Victoria . . . I want to . . ."

He trailed off, and though he didn't die, he was certainly going into shock and would die very soon if something wasn't done. If anything could even be done for that wound. Part of me figured that even if Superman and Batman showed up right now and saved us, Gabe would still die before we could ever get to a hospital.

I spun around, teeth bared.

"Don't even think it." Walt swung his gun back to me and aimed it at my chest. "I won't end you so graciously. I'll put it in your dick. The next one will go in your stomach. Your buddy may die fairly quickly but you'll go slow as molasses. Now dig the fucking hole so

I can have my fun and then get on with my night. Told you, I want
to check this off my list."

"Where are you taking Victoria?"

Gabe kicked, gurgled, went still. But I could still hear his breath
making the blood bubble up. I turned away, sick to my stomach.

"Um, I don't remember saying I'd tell you a damn thing. Did I?
Let me think back . . . something about digging your own grave,
shooting your dick? Nope. Nothing about chitchatting about that
whore in there. Now stick that shovel back in the dirt." He aimed
the gun at my dick now. "I'm counting to three. One. Two . . ."

I bent down and picked up the shovel again. At my feet, Gabe
was bleeding out, his throat torn open. I was pretty sure there was
no hope for him now. And what was worse, I couldn't think of a
single thing to say to him in his last moments. Here he was, dying,
knowing his true love had just been raped and was getting taken
somewhere for who knew what, and I couldn't say a damn thing to
make it better. All I could do was tell myself it wasn't fair.

"Dig! Now!"

I jammed the shovel back into the earth and tossed more dirt
over my shoulder. Maybe if I dug slowly enough I could think of
a way to get out of this.

Bob came walking out of the garage a second later, stabbing a
finger at his watch. "Yo, Walt, it's getting late. What the hell is taking you? We're supposed to get her there in twenty minutes. It's
gonna take longer than that just to drive there." He stooped and
looked at the scene. "What's with the digging? Is that guy dead?
Just shoot them both for fuck's sake."

"Making them dig their own graves. Like in the movies."

Bob shook his head. "Really? Well, that's cool and all but I don't
wanna get gypped on my money. Time is money, right?"

"So then take her. I'll finish these two . . . er, one . . . and meet
up with you. I'll take Roger's car. I wanna do this."

"You sure? You got this under control?"

"Does it look like I don't? I wanna see his dying face looking
back at me when I start burying him. I'm feeling sick tonight."

"Actually, that's some cold shit. I wanna see that, too. Maybe
I'll stay and get a front row seat."

"No! Get that bitch delivered and get my share if they dole it out. I'll be there soon enough. And don't even think about skimming from my cash."

Bob studied Gabe as he lay dying in the dirt. A smile crossed his face, like someone had just told him a real funny story. "Okay, but what about lighting the house up? I was gonna do it right now. The gas and rags are all set and everything. The usual MO. We gotta do it"

"I'll take care of it. Don't worry about anything. That one's almost dead there" —he pointed to Gabe— "and Roger here is a fast digger, ain't you, Roger? I'll set the house burning and only be a few minutes behind. Now get going already. You're ruining my mood."

"Fine. But I want that hat." He plucked the Red Sox cap off Walt's head, put it on, and walked back to the garage. A minute later I heard the SUV pulling onto the street and driving toward the highway.

"Where are you taking her?"

"Roger, if I wanted to hear your voice I'd beat you with my cock and listen to you beg for mercy. Keep digging!"

I thought about ways to escape for the next couple of minutes, but nothing good came to me. I thought about how I'd gotten out of the cuffs in Skinny Man's basement, about how I'd swung that ax into his forehead and freed myself from captivity, but it wasn't really giving me any ideas. I wasn't alone and there wasn't any ax nearby. Again, I figured I could throw the shovel, but I'd have to bet on him being a lousy shot . . . which I already knew he wasn't from the way he'd taken out Gabe. All I could think of was I had to keep him talking.

"You're gonna kill me anyway, so just tell me where you're taking her."

"You sound like your friend there. You fags rehearse this speech?"

"Think about it. If you're gonna do something bad to her, wouldn't you want me to die knowing what you're doing. It would make me crazy. It would hurt me. That's your style, right?"

Walt chuckled and waved away a mosquito with the gun. "Oh yeah, like I'm just gonna tell you where she's going. Let me explain something about this business I'm in. Rule number one: don't talk. Rule number two: don't fucking talk. Rule number three: don't.

Fucking. Talk."

"What was rule number two again?"

He snickered. "I think that was the one where if you talk again I shoot you in the fucking teeth."

"You're taking her to someone? Who?"

"Your mother."

"You're a long way from my mom's house."

"Loose lips sink ships. You ever hear that? I don't need to know where she ends up or what happens to her. I don't really fucking care. I already got what I wanted from her. Now I get paid to deliver her. That's it. If you ask another question, I'm gonna fire another round. Capiche?"

Somewhere in my mind I could hear Tooth giving me a hard time for not trying to fight this guy. *He's a pussy, Roger, he uses a gun. Without that gun he's nothing.*

Beside me, Gabe gurgled and I could hear him taking a piss. Human's let out their bowels and bladders when they die, but I tried not to think about it. Somewhere out near the foothills I heard a coyote cry out. It was like a primeval siren in the desert night, some kind of battle cry that stood my hairs on end. For a second my brain was able to grasp the severity of my situation, how I was going to die out here in this bleak desert where my parents would never find me. Victoria, who'd already been violated in the worst way possible, would probably end up in a similar situation. And for what? I still had no idea. I needed to keep him talking, wait for a moment that would give me an upper hand. I couldn't believe— wouldn't believe—that after all I'd been through, after surviving Skinny Man, I'd get killed by a scumbag like Walt.

At least not like this. I mean, I could understand getting mugged by a guy like Walt in a dark alley, but to succumb to another round of torture first from a moron as unimaginative as him…come on, world, where's your sense of respect?

"You want to know something about your friend, about that girlie in there? I think she came. Yeah, I think she liked it. Ain't that a killer?"

It was all I could do to keep digging and not rush at him. My hand gripped the shaft of the shovel so tightly I could see the whites of my knuckles in the darkness.

"That's right," he continued. "Funny how bitches have them rape fantasies. They all like it, like to be forced into it. Want you to shove yourself into them as they scream and hit you and say no no no. But they like it, oh yes they do. Fuck a bitch enough times she'll tell you eventually how she wants to be taken by force. I'd recommend you try yourself some rape, but shit, only thing you're gonna shove your meat into is worms. Now don't you look at me like that. Keep that shovel moving."

I wouldn't know anything about rough sex, not having slept with many girls, but I sure as shit knew Walt had a skewed view of how women work. Tooth used to tell me that some girls liked to engage in weird fantasies where some strange man would have his way with them, but the thing is, it was all done in the midst of fun and respect and trust. What had been done to Victoria was evil. The result of a sickness that too many men in this world take pride in, a disconnect that they use to give themselves power over a gender they perceive as weak. That's all it is in the end: a pathetic and weak display of cowardice for a cheap thrill. I hoped Walt and his idiot friends burned in Hell for it.

"How far down is that," he asked me, "four feet? That's good enough, it'll cover over. Drop the shovel."

I looked up at Walt, saw the moon in the sky behind him, like a rind of rotted cantaloupe keeping watch over us. Is this it? I wondered. I'll hear a loud bang and then black will overtake me?

"Was it good for you?" I asked.

"Nah. I'm impatient, and you took a bit longer than I expected."

"You said I was a good digger."

"I say a lot of shit. Don't mean I always agree with it. You dig like my grandma taking a shit—slow and hopeful, and in the end all you expel is hot air."

"She must have been a lovely lady."

"Best pork ribs this side of Texas. But you tell me . . . how's it feel to be standing in your own grave?"

"Don't suppose you'd take money or anything? Forget about everything that happened here tonight. What's your price?"

"Now that is a sad sight, a man begging for his life with money he can't possibly have. My price? There's more zeros in my price than even I'm able count."

"Then that's works in my favor since I'm betting you can't count beyond two."

He paused. Then: "You know, I've killed a dozen men in my day, and only two had the balls you got, kid. But what amazes me about having balls is that it brings out the comedian in people. It's pretty damn cheap and erases any sense of bravado you could show me in your final seconds. I mean, if you wanted me to feel like you were truly tough, spitting at me or giving me the finger would go a lot further. But bad jokes just get lost on the wind."

"So I'll take that as yes, you can't count."

"I'm getting paid well for this. More than you can give me. You know every time Bob grunted when he fucked that bitch in there? Imagine a thousand dollars for every one. I stopped counting after one hundred. Besides," he patted his jacket pocket and I heard keys jingle, "I got your car now, so I'll consider that your payment."

I debated telling him about the stupidity of driving around in a pinstriped Camaro that would sooner or later be reported missing by either my parents or Barry or someone, but realized it might be the only way he ever got caught.

"Now," he said, "since you're such a funny guy, I'm changing how we do this."

"Meaning?"

"Meaning that I'm not gonna shoot you. See, not only have I never seen a man dig his own grave, but I ain't never seen one get buried alive either. I want you totally conscious when I do this." He gave one of those smirks that's supposed to convey his cleverness but really just made him look like an imbecile. "So do me a kindness and toss the shovel to the side. Then get on your stomach."

My mind was racing, my eyes scanning my surroundings. I couldn't think of any way out of this short of just rushing him and taking a bullet in the stomach. Probably wouldn't kill me, but at least I wouldn't be focused on suffocating under four feet of dirt.

Now would be a good time for some help, Tooth, I thought. *If you're up there looking down and haven't pissed off the Big Guy, I could use a distraction.*

"Hey, there's no invite coming. Toss the shovel down or I shoot your kneecaps."

"But you just said—"

"Forget what I say, just do as I say!"

"Well that makes sense. Don't I get any last words?"

"No. Lay down." He held his free hand out and motioned for me to lay the shovel down.

That mosquito that had been flittering around Walt's head landed on his nose.

It sat like a witch's mole on the bulbous flesh.

I slid my hand around the top of the shovel's shaft. "Fine. Here."

C'mon, bite him, I thought.

It was a subconscious move on his part. A meaningless little swipe at the pest trying to suck his blood. But like last time, he used the gun to wave it away.

I launched the shovel at him.

"Fuck!" he yelled as he tried to dodge it.

It hit him in square in the face. He staggered back and raised the gun.

I was out of the hole and charging. There was a loud bang and something whizzed by my ear. I slid into his legs like someone stealing bases.

He came down on top of me and I wrapped my arms around his neck and squeezed for all I was worth.

He kicked and tried to get the gun around to my body, but I caught his wrist and jammed my thumb into the tender spot between his tendons. He lost the grip on the gun and let it dangle on his finger by the trigger guard. "Motherfucker!"

My arms blazed with pain as I tightened my grip around his windpipe.

The gun came up handle-first and struck me in my broken nose, making my eyes tear up. It was such an intense pain I almost let go of him to roll over and wail. But I kept squeezing, kept telling myself it was either that or die.

Walt was bigger than me by at least sixty pounds, so he finally stood up, taking me with him. I wrapped my legs around him and kicked him in the groin, hanging on like a kid getting a piggyback ride.

With a mighty grunt he threw himself down on top of me, knocking the wind from my lungs.

When we landed he dropped the gun. I reached out and

grabbed it, gasping for breath, just as his size–twelve boot caught me in the ribs and rolled me back several feet.

With no breath in my lungs, blurred vision, and what felt like a cracked rib, I raised the gun and fired.

His body ran right into me and knocked the gun from my hand. Sent me backwards again. But the bullet had found its target.

Right through his left eye.

He stopped moving, stood still, teetering, his one good eye staring at me. A mosquito—maybe the same one—swooped in and landed in the bloody mess where his eyeball had been.

Somehow, he managed to bend over and pick up the gun. I'd heard of people getting shot in the head and living but never figured they be lucid enough to keep fighting. My jaw dropped.

He pointed the gun at me. A line of drool slipped from his mouth and hung in a silky ribbon from his lower lip.

My last thought was, *Victoria.*

BANG!

I flinched. My heart just about ripped from my chest. But I felt no pain.

Instead, I watched as the back of Walt's head blew out in a dark, shadowy bloom. He fell straight back into the four-foot-deep grave I'd dug and went still.

I turned to my left, saw a shadowy figure holding a rifle and walking toward me.

"Oh shit oh shit oh shit. I was aiming for his legs, I swear." It was Leslie. "I was shaking and I tried to raise it just a little. I swear. You gotta believe me."

Chapter 10

I got up and found my breath. "Thank God, you're a bad shot."

"Holy shit I killed him. Oh my God this is not good. I saw him pointing the gun at you and . . ."

I found the strength to walk toward him, limping and wheezing. I held my hands out so he could see I didn't have a weapon. "He was gonna kill me, Leslie."

Leslie raised the rifle and pointed it at me. "Stop right there. I don't know what this shit's all about but I don't want any of it."

"Leslie, look at me. Look at my face. I can barely move. I'm not gonna give you any trouble. But please listen. Three men just raped my friend, killed her boyfriend, and just took her somewhere to do . . . I don't know. I need to—"

"Who are you?"

"Stay on target, Leslie. Do you hear what I'm saying? I have to go right now and find her before she's killed. I know what this must look like but you gotta believe I didn't come up here to cause trouble. So please stop aiming the gun at me."

For the first time Leslie spotted Gabe's body over by the grave. "Who's that?"

"That's the boyfriend I just told you about. They made us dig our graves. They're kidnappers and rapists. You following? Look at my hands and clothes, Leslie. I'm covered in dirt because I just dug that fucking grave. Tell me you're following me?"

Leslie nodded, but he looked pretty damn confused. "How do I know any of this is true? And why didn't you mention it before?"

"Didn't know if I was onto something or just being panicky. It's a long story. So here's the thing. I really really need to go. My name is Roger Huntington. These guys are in a white SUV. One of them has a tattoo of an eagle on his head. He said he was in the joint once, so they probably can find his photo in a prison database somewhere. You can tell the cops all that."

"What the—! You can't leave! The cops will think I killed these guys myself. I mean, I killed that one there but I didn't mean to and I thought I was stopping something—"

"You did. And I thank you."

"But . . . but . . . how are you gonna find her? Don't *you* want to talk to the cops and—"

"They'll spend more time questioning me than looking. I sort of have a . . . a history."

"What's that mean?"

"Nothing to worry about. But let's just say I'm on record."

"I knew it. There's more to this shit than you're telling me."

"It's not like that. Just, sort of, got into a fight a while back."

"Yeah, well, ain't we all. I got nabbed for a bar fight a few years ago. Apparently it's uncool for a man like me to like Kelly Clarkson."

"I don't think it is."

"Man, can she sing. Sweet as an angel."

"Leslie, please."

Finally he lowered the gun. "Fucking-A, I was just looking for the damn kids. They're still out on their motorbikes somewhere. I hear all these voices and figure I'll see if this SUV you mentioned been cutting across my property like you said—"

"Leslie, I don't have time for a conversation. I really do have to go! Can you call the cops and take care of this? My friend is in real danger. Look, I have a card."

I patted my back pocket, but realized the goons had taken my wallet. Probably still had it. "Shit. Okay, I don't have a card. You're gonna have to trust me, because I'm walking to my car. My friend Victoria Watson has been kidnapped. Her boyfriend Gabe was shot by that fucker in the hole there. They can match the bullet and gun and powder burns and all that shit. Her car is still parked out at the lake a ways back. That's what you tell the cops. So you either have the gist of this or you'll have to shoot me in my back."

I took my car keys and Walt's cell phone from Walt's pocket and headed toward the driveway. The phone looked cheap and plastic and disposable. Leslie, to his somewhat uneducated credit, let me pass. Just before I rounded the house to the front he called after me.

"Hey, Roger, if this is true—"

"It's true," I called back.

"Then kill the bastards."

I nodded. I don't know if he saw me and I didn't care. This was a race against the clock and I had no idea how to even begin finding out where'd they'd gone.

I got in my car and started it up. Next, I took out Walt's cell phone and hit redial. The name said GOLDILOCKS. I'd heard Walt mention that name in the house. Meant nothing to me but at least it was the beginning of a trail.

The phone on the other end rang and rang and then just clicked off. I scrolled through the call log and saw that every name was in Mother Goose code: GOLDILOCKS, BIG BAD WOLF, HUMPTY DUMPTY, BO PEEP, JACK HORNER, etcetera.

I tried calling a couple other numbers and got the same response. They would ring and ring and then go dead.

I got out of the car and looked at the street to see if I could find those tire tracks again, but it was too dark now to make out anything discernable.

"Shit." I got back in and drove.

As I sped down the street toward Leslie's house I scrolled through the phone's functions and found a photo of Victoria. I couldn't tell where it had been taken because the background was just a white wall, but she was smiling, partly looking the other way, unaware she was being spied on.

That did not make me feel good. They'd been watching her for a while. It made me feel sick.

I cut the car across Leslie's property once again and headed for that desolate road. I wanted to go back to Victoria's car one last time and look for anything that might help me find them.

The whole way there I racked my brain for anything they might have said about where they were going. Nothing came to mind. All I saw were images of Victoria splayed across that weight bench having her dignity and pride stripped from her.

When I got to the lake the water was so dark it looked like the night sky had fallen and spread out across the ground. In other circumstances I might have considered it romantic, but this night it was just ominous. All the other cars had gone for the day. Victoria's

car was where she'd left it. I wondered if the cops I'd called earlier
had ever showed up, maybe even tried to find the owner of the
abandoned vehicle, but seriously doubted it.

Nothing about the car had changed since I last saw it. The
handprint was still on the glass. The cigarette butts were still lit-
tered on the ground. I tried the door but it was locked.

This was a dead end. What the hell was I thinking? Leslie was
right: I needed to just go talk to the authorities.

But I knew Victoria could be dead by the time they did anything about this.

I tried that Goldilocks number again. Nothing but ringing.

I hung up and dialed Teddy in New Hampshire. How the hell
I even remembered his number is beyond me. I'm so used to just
hitting the auto dial on my cell phone. I guess we'd talked enough
over the years it had lodged in my subconscious.

"Teddy, it's me."

"Roger! What the hell happened? What number is this?"

"In a second. Listen, a friend of mine was kidnapped."

"What? Are you okay?"

"I think my nose is broken and maybe a rib, too. I'm in some
serious pain here. Did you trace the call like I said?"

"Hang on, I need to get a pen and pad." The line went silent for
a minute and then Teddy was back. "Okay. I couldn't trace the call
because I don't know what carrier you're on. And unless you're on
one I have a friend at I'd need a warrant anyway. But I did call a
Detective Chavez out there who said he'd try to call around and
ping your number."

"I didn't see any cops."

"I don't know what to tell you. It's not always accurate. They
can get a location off cell phone calls but if the tower was a ways
off the search area could be pretty wide."

"Well, nevermind. I found the guys who kidnapped my friend."

"And?"

"And they killed her boyfriend and raped her. They were gonna
kill me but I got away. I need to find her."

"I can't believe I'm hearing this."

"It's not a joke, Teddy. I'm so angry and scared right now I'm
shaking."

"Did you call the cops?"

"Someone else is doing it for me. I had to leave. I think they're gonna kill her."

"Please don't tell me you ran from a crime scene. That's no good. Is anyone else dead?"

"One of the rapists. Guy named Walt. I didn't do it, though I tried. Tried like hell."

"This is bad, Roger. They have procedures to deal with this kind of thing and you're gonna make it worse."

"Teddy, you know as soon as they run my background they're gonna keep me under lock and key. I can't do that right now."

"So I'm helping a wanted man right now?"

"Yep. Pretty much."

Teddy sighed long and hard. "Ok. Fine. I hate my job most days anyway. What do you need from me?"

"There's a number on this phone. I called it but no one picks up. Can you find out who it belongs to?"

"I can try. But it's the same thing again. I may not get squat."

"Just try." I relayed the number to him.

"Okay, give me a few minutes and I'll call my contacts, see if they can help. I'll call you back at this number."

"Thanks, Teddy."

"And I'm calling Detective Chavez back as well. I need to report all of this. Don't suppose you have an address where the dead guy is?"

"I didn't look. But tell them a guy named Leslie is supposed to call, too. I'm sure they can put two and two together."

"Okay, sit tight and try to stay out of trouble."

"No promises."

I put the phone in my pocket and walked around Victoria's car some more. For some reason I felt there should be a clue here, like there always is in movies. Some piece of paper with an address on it or a matchbook from a bar or something.

Standing next to that bloody handprint got all sorts of scenarios going in my mind. How they'd rape Victoria again if I couldn't find her. Rape her and then kill her . . .

I'd feed her to the dog and then rape the dog's shit the next day.

It was Skinny Man, back in my mind. I closed my eyes, clenched my fists and counted to ten. When I was done I opened my eyes and saw him dancing around the empty parking lot, laughing his stupid laugh. Even though I knew he wasn't real, was a figment of my traumatized imagination, I still wanted to rush at him and beat him to death.

Sad how all these girls die around you, huh, Roger? Fuck me, you should just cut their heads off instead of trying to make friends with them. Save everyone sometime.

"Shut up!"

My phone rang. The digital clock said ten minutes had passed. It felt like an eternity.

"Teddy?"

"Hey, I traced the call. It was easy because it's a payphone. You got a pen and paper?"

"Yeah, hang on."

I went back to my car and searched frantically but couldn't find a pen. Instead I grabbed one of my paintbrushes and put some black paint on it. "Okay, go."

Teddy relayed the address and I scrawled it across the blue sky of my painting from earlier in the day. The piece was ruined now, but in light of these events it couldn't have meant less to me. I'd paint another one if I ever got out of this situation with a sane mind.

"I need you to MapQuest me," I told him. "I'm at a place called Corazon del Agua."

I heard him clicking away on his computer. A minute later he had directions. I painted them over the grass.

"Okay, I'm going," I told him.

"Roger, I'm serious here. Be careful and don't engage anyone. You find anything you call 911. In fact, here's Chavez's cell phone number."

I obliged him and painted the numbers on the canvas.

"Got it."

"I'm calling him back myself," Teddy said. "I need to tell him about all of this. You'll probably get there before he does. It's the best I can do. You know I'm gonna vouch for you and explain what you told me but just so you know, cops will extend courtesies to one another but only so far."

"Yeah, I get it. Talk soon."

"Here's hoping."

I spun back once and looked for Skinny Man, but he was gone.

Chapter 11

Twenty minutes later I was standing in the parking lot of a liquor store off of Gardenia Avenue staring at the payphone on the wall outside the door.

A Middle Eastern man was working the counter, selling a six-pack to some college kids. I waited for them to leave before approaching.

"Help you?" he asked me.

"Maybe. Did you see anyone on that payphone earlier today?"

"Lots of people. Why? You look too young to be a cop?"

"I'm looking for someone."

"I don't know what to tell you, lots of people use that phone. You wanna buy something?"

"No. Okay, yes. Here, I'll get this Snickers bar."

He rang it up and charged me a dollar-fifty, which I found a bit steep for candy I wasn't even going to eat; I just wanted to see if I could get more out of him. Luckily, I had a five in my pocket to broker the ruse.

"You hear anyone talking about kidnapping a girl on the phone?"

He laughed. "You serious? What is this a fucking TV show? Son, I can't hear what people say on it. I don't pay attention. I don't even own it. Belongs to an outside company. That's all I can tell you."

"Are there video cameras outside?"

"Did you see any? No, just over the counter here."

An older woman walked in and stood behind me at the counter. "You have Virginia Slims," she asked, rudely cutting off my conversation.

I decided to stop bothering the guy and went out to the payphone. There was a big blue redial button on it so I dropped fifty cents in the slot and hit it. It told me the number I was trying to reach had been disconnected and no further number was available. Not that it meant it was a number associated with the people I was looking for, but it sent a shiver up my spine anyway.

I was about to get back in my car and cry when I noticed a small painting hanging on the wall inside near one of the coolers. I damn near ran inside and knocked that rude lady over as she was exiting with her smokes.

"Hey, careful!" the clerk yelled.

Ignoring him, I shoved aside a Captain Morgan display and took the painting off the wall. A plein air piece. Three palm trees and a little hut with surfboards leaning against it. My knees felt weak.

My initials were still scrawled on the bottom of the canvas.

I'd painted this piece about six months ago and gave it to Barry to sell.

"You buy this?" I asked the clerk, putting the painting on the counter.

"The fuck, kid. Go put that back!"

"I painted this. It's my painting. Did you buy it?"

"You painted that?"

"Yes. It's one of mine. I sell at Goldstein Gallery. Did you buy it?"

"Me? No, got it as a gift, kind of, from Barry."

"You know Barry? Barry Goldstein?"

"Yeah, he lives down the street. He gave it to me one night, said he wanted some booze but was out of cash. I said okay because it adds some flair. Why? You want me to pay you for it?"

"No . . . no. I just . . . . Where does Barry live? He's my employer. I need to talk to him."

"Down the road there, around the corner. I don't know what house but he comes in sometimes."

I swallowed hard and took a step back from the counter. "Tell me he didn't come in here today and use the payphone."

The clerk kind of tilted his head. I don't think he wanted to tell me what I knew he was going to say, but he did it anyway. "Yeah, he was in a little earlier. Said he was on his way home for dinner."

"And he used the payphone?"

"I think so, yes. Not really sure. I think it was him."

I was out the door before he could say anything else. My Camaro spun out in the parking lot as I sped to the nearest side street.

"Keep it together," I whispered, "don't lose your shit yet."

Skinny Man appeared on the passenger seat beside me. *No, lose it. Use it. You know what you're good at. Let the blood flow.*

"I don't have time for you right now, asshole."

So what? I have plenty of time for you. For your friends and girlies. I want to play.

I swung my arm into him and hit the seat. The action made me swerve to avoid a car parked on the side of the road; when I straightened out the apparition was gone.

"Don't lose it, Roger. Stay on target."

I went another two blocks before I spotted Barry's BMW parked in the driveway of a two-story house with a good-sized front yard. He was apparently doing all right for himself financially. And here I was living in a crappy studio apartment. It just made me even angrier.

I parked on the side of the road and walked up the front steps, knocked on the door. From the other side I heard the familiar voice of the man who spent his days trying to threaten me. "Hang on!"

A second later the door opened and Barry stood there in his customary button-down and khakis. "Roger? What the hell are you doing here? It's late."

Hopefully not too late, I thought. I stepped inside, right around him. He turned and followed.

"You okay?" he asked. "What happened to your face? Your nose is a mess. Your eyes . . ."

I studied the art on his walls. Lots of cheap landscapes and the occasional photorealism piece. None of my stuff was hanging up anywhere.

"I said, 'are you okay?'"

"Are *you* okay?" I replied.

"What's that mean? Stop pacing. What happened to you?"

I stood right in front of him. Rage was making me curl my lips. "Where's Victoria?"

"I don't know. Why? She took off today with your painting and never came back. I called her phone and told her I was firing her if she didn't have a good excuse. I may just fire her anyway. What's wrong with you?"

It was a good answer, it sounded legit.

I tried a new tactic. Cheap and old, but I needed to know what he'd say. I pretended to lighten up. "Sorry, Barry. I'm in some trouble and I lost my phone. I was searching for a payphone but couldn't find one. Just by luck I was driving around here and saw your car. You'd think there'd be a payphone around here."

"You want to use mine? What kind of trouble are you in? Tell me what happened to your face."

"Nothing big, just a private client thing."

He studied my broken nose as he talked. "Working around me. Thought I had your contract."

"I'm free to work outside of the gallery, you know that. Where's the nearest payphone?"

"How the hell should I know? I have a phone, just use mine."

How the hell should I know? There it was, the lie I needed.

I grabbed him by his shirtfront and slammed him into the wall. The painting near his head fell from its hook and clattered on the hardwood floor.

"Roger! What the fu—"

"Shut up. Who'd you call on the phone at the liquor store?"

"The hell are you talking about?"

"Tell me or I swear I'll punch your teeth down your throat."

"I didn't call anyone."

"Bullshit. The clerk saw you." I took the cell phone from my pocket and held it up. "You call this?"

For the briefest of seconds I saw recognition in his eyes. "I don't know—"

I slammed him backwards again, smacked his head against the wall. This time he shoved back, but I kneed him in the balls. He sank to his knees, hands holding his dick. I lifted his head up and pressed the phone to his face. "You call this? It's a simple question."

"I'm calling the police. You'll never work for—"

I hit him in the mouth with the cell phone. He grunted and cowered beneath me. Seeing him like that made me cringe, gave me flashbacks of killing Skinny Man. But in some distant part of me I was only beginning to understand, it felt damn good.

"I'll ask one more time, Barry, then I'm throwing punches. Tell me what's going on. I know you were on the payphone at the liquor store. I know that payphone called this phone. I know this phone was in the possession of a man who kidnapped Victoria, your employee. That person who had her, by the way, is very much dead now. Fill in the rest, Goldilocks."

Now he looked up at me and met my eyes in a different light.

I said, "You're involved in this, aren't you, Goldilocks? Too many coincidences here. It adds up."

He chuckled and leaned back against the wall. "You don't know what you're getting into, Roger."

"Too late, I'm already in it. Where's Victoria?"

"I can't tell you that."

"Why?"

"Because they'll kill me. And they'll kill you."

"They already tried and failed. No more secrets, Barry. No more vague nonsense."

"Then kill me. That won't get you anything."

"I'm weighing that outcome based on your cooperation."

"Ha! You talk tough, Roger. Did you really kill someone today? I doubt it."

"Big fucker named Walt. One of your three bears. Yeah, he's dead. Want to try me again?"

The name meant something to him, I could tell. He remained silent though. I decided to let him know I meant business.

"You get things for people, Barry. Remember? That's what you do . . . you get things for people. There's no way you can afford this house and that car and all the shit you have just by selling my paintings. I know the rents in this town. They're steep, too steep for the way you're living. This phone connects you to some very bad people. There's a camera outside that store. Bet we could play connect the phone call time stamps pretty easily. Figure out how you manage this lifestyle."

That part about the camera was a lie, but I was willing to play the bluff to scare him. And, for the hell of it, I punched him square in the mouth. His lip split and poured blood down the front of his shirt. My hand throbbed from the force of the blow, but I didn't let on.

"Stop hitting me!"

"Where is she? What's going on?"

"Roger, you really don't want to get involved in this."

"Try me, Goldilocks. Next time, use a name not so close to your own."

"I didn't come up with it. They did. They pick something close to your character. I'm Jewish, so they thought it was funny."

I pulled my hand back, balled it up, and went to hit him again.

"Wait! Okay. Dammit. I don't know where she is exactly, only that she was being taken up to Rancho Vaiella. Some estate."

"Give me a name."

"Worthington."

"You're lying."

"Of course I am. I'm not going to tell you their real names, idiot." He started laughing.

"You're the idiot." I left him lying on the ground and went out to my car. I'd always dreaded the idea that I'd have to use my gun on someone, but tonight I was feeling more than justified. As I walked back up the walkway Skinny Man was there, smiling at me. I walked through him like he was smoke. When I returned, Barry was crawling toward the phone on the end table near the sofa. I kicked him in the stomach and he rolled into the wall.

"Gonna shoot me now?" he asked.

"Yes."

BANG!

I shot him in the knee.

Man, how he wailed. The shot echoed throughout the entire house. My time was limited now; neighbors would be calling the cops.

"Get up." I hauled him to his feet as he screamed in protest and dragged him into the nearest hallway, pulled him down it until I found what I was looking for.

His home office.

I shoved him into the chair in front of his computer. Blood from his leg was pooling on the floor. "Turn it on."

He was crying, tears running down his cheeks, the pain of his shattered knee cap too much to bear. "It's already on, asshole." He tapped the mouse to bring it out of sleep mode.

"Call up sales from the gallery. I know you, Barry, you're an anal jackass so I know you've got records here. Call up everything."

I placed the gun against his other kneecap. "Wanna go for two?"

"They're going to kill you. And these people do not kill quickly."

"Do it now."

He obliged me. The screen cut to an invoice record for the last year's worth of gallery sales. There were two addresses listed in Rancho Vaiella.

"Which one is it?" I asked, cocking the hammer on the gun still pressed to his good knee.

"Figure it out yourself." His right arm came up so fast I barely had time to see it. The carved rock paperweight that had been next to the keyboard caught me in the neck and knocked me backwards.

Reflexively I fired the gun but the bullet hit the computer tower under the desk. Sparks flew out like cheap fireworks. Barry was up and hobbling and grabbing something from the drawer of the desk.

I saw the gun come up at me just as I hit the wall and fell to my ass. The bullet from his gun went over my head and shattered the mirror clock above me. As the shards rained down I fired my own gun and saw half of Barry's neck explode outward. He dropped to his knees in front of me, staring a hole through me as he fell forward into my lap.

A few shards of reflective clock face twinkled as they fell from my hair to the back of Barry's head. The warm blood from his bullet wound seeped into the crotch of my pants.

"Sonofabitch," I said, rolling the body off me. My neck ached something fierce. In what was left of the shattered mirror clock above me I caught a glimpse of my appearance. Black eyes, purple swollen nose, red lump on my neck. I looked like hell.

"Why'd you do that, Barry?" I kicked him to make sure he was dead. Dr. Marsh would not be surprised to learn I didn't feel much of anything right now—not that I had plans to see her anymore.

I looked back at the computer, saw the bullet hole in the tower. The monitor was black. Shit.

It didn't matter. I'd seen the address for the house in Rancho Vaiella. I had a name now. I knew the man, because everyone knew the man. And I'd seen him in the gallery before . . . flirting with Victoria.

Marshall Aldridge. He owned the chain of Golden Sun Spas, which was really just a euphemism for plastic surgery and cosmetic makeover clinics. He was in the news at least once a month. Local

philanthroper, sat on the board of the Art Museum, right wing con-
servative. The usual for these assholes that lived in Rancho Vaiella.
Worse, he bought my stuff.

Chapter 12

Okay, when I mentioned I didn't feel anything about killing Barry, that was kind of a lie. I felt a ton of things, all swirling around my head as I drove.

Barry marked the second time in my life I had killed someone. Most of you know the first time—Skinny Man. Shoved an ax into his head and split his skull. That had me fucked up for years. Still does. The scary thing about killing Barry was that it almost felt familiar.

I can't describe the feeling that reels inside you when you take a life. It's bigger than words. It's why I keep that crucifix in my glove compartment. Because there's a deifying quality to killing. Not a good one, don't get me wrong. There's nothing good about it at all, even if it's self defense. You've just ended a life, the most precious gift of humanity. If you believe in God, and I wrestle with that still sometimes, then you've undone the work of a higher power. We're not meant to have such a right.

I suppose if you believe in simple evolution, then you believe we are the only gods that exist. That we are the most intelligent beings on the planet—what a scary thought that is—and therefore have no one to answer to.

Then why both the first time I killed and this time, did I feel like I needed to atone for a sin?

Because I know the difference between a superhero and a supervillain. Cardinal rule: you don't kill. You bring villains to justice. That's why Batman, Spider-Man, Green Lantern, the X-Men, all my boyhood heroes . . . that's why they have endured for so long and are so important today. Because people need to know that the notion of a hero is still worthy. It's like believing in a different type of higher power. We need these stories because we need to believe that society is not just a newsreel of twentieth century archetypes:

rapists, murderers, arsonists, thieves, pedophiles, mind-warpers. Justice is noble, but flawed, yet heroes at least strive to prove justice is attainable. They let us know we still have a semblance of humanity left in us.

I am not a superhero. I have taken lives, and I have learned to be okay with it. Why? Because the real supervillains are not men made of blue light or beings from other planets: they're humans who think they're gods. They are men who live above society's rules. When Batman brings a true psychopath to justice, said villain is given a padded room and three square meals a day. And if you read comics like I do, you know they just break out and do it again. This is why justice is a hero's pipedream. It's why superheroes don't really exist.

I stopped trying to be a hero when I killed Skinny Man, when I failed to bring him to justice but instead put him down like a rabid animal. He deserved it. And no one argued against my actions. What does that make me? I am more Darth Vader than Luke Skywalker, more Rorschach than Nite Owl. I give into my rage and pain, because I have come to accept the end result. That some people, plain and simple, are a cancer. And if we let them persist, they continue to destroy. It's not justice, it's a new reform.

This is wrong and I know it, but I deal with it. This is why I don't wear the crucifix, but take it out and hold it, ask for forgiveness, listen for an answer that either doesn't come or that I cannot recognize. I don't know if I will be forgiven in the end, but for now, I know I can live with it.

One more thing. When I killed Skinny Man, part of me died and was replaced by something darker and stronger. Some kind of emotional wall made of iron and steel and Teflon, something that coats my soul and makes it possible to be okay with what just happened to Barry. I am able to shut down the need to cry and bang my head against the wall. I am able to lock those feelings away.

I can feel new pieces of the wall growing inside me, erasing what little bit of the old Roger managed to hang on these last ten years. I feel like something new, something wrong, something broken.

But sadly, I don't mind it.

●●●

I drove to the 5 and headed north. The blood on my pants was starting to congeal and turn cold, like day-old oatmeal. The knot on my neck was swelling up worse and I was waiting for it to cut off my breathing, but thankfully the bruise was growing outward. My eyesight was still bit blurry from my busted nose.

And I smelled pretty ripe. Trust me, deodorant is an understated invention.

I felt a little bit more alive in a twisted way that would have psychologists scribbling warnings in their pads. Maybe it was the drive, maybe it was the excitement of death still fresh in my mind. Maybe I was just cuckoo for Coco Puffs.

I didn't know if the cops were on the way to Barry's house or not. Eventually someone would find him and put two and two together. I hadn't bothered to clean up and I didn't really care. If there was any justice in the world his corpse would rot and never get a proper burial. Right now, Victoria was my priority and everything else could be explained later.

Maybe.

Hopefully.

Man, I stank.

I flipped open the cell phone and called Teddy. He answered right away.

"What's going on?"

"Nothing you want to hear. I think I know where Victoria is. Maybe."

"Where?"

"I need you to call the cops and get people to Marshall Aldridge's house. Tell them they have a kidnapped girl there." I gave him the address and hoped he'd hang up, but he was too smart to do that.

"You're headed there, aren't you?"

"Yup. Don't suppose you'll MapQuest it for me?" "Don't do this, Roger."

"Have to. Will you get me directions?"

"No. And why? You're going to end up dead or in too much trouble for anyone to help you out of."

"Gotta do it anyway."

"Why?"

"Because I always wait for him to kill her. I never save her. But not this time."

"What the hell are you talking about? Roger, whatever it is you're going through right now this is not the answer."

"You're wasting time not calling the cops."

There was a moment of silence. Then: "I'm calling you right back."

The road was pretty open this time of night. Not like rush hour, where you moved at a snail's pace. The gun lay on the seat next to me, my new co-pilot. Sad, in a real way. We Americans are so used to solving problems with guns that we tend to forget the whole part about how they bring about death. I suppose if I was a ninja I'd have settled for a sword, something more honorable, but I didn't have that ability. And without the gun Victoria would likely die. I hated that gun, hated every gun and every weapon that man had ever learned to wield.

Hated that I was good with it.

My easel and half-finished paintings were still in the backseat. I wondered what other painters carried firearms. I wondered if "alligator wrestler" would be a less stressful job.

I went another ten miles north and the phone rang.

"Teddy?"

"I called the cops. They're on their way now. They know who this guy is and said they're not pleased with having to bother him. I had to give them your information, too, Roger. I advise you to co-operate to the fullest extent—"

"Gladly. Just want to make sure she's still alive."

"You're still going there?"

"I already said that. Even without your directions."

"I'm not helping you get into more trouble. I can't help you any further. You understand?"

The phone beeped. I pulled it away and saw the battery light flashing. "Phone's dying. Thanks for everything."

"Roger!"

I hung up, feeling strangely more focused now than I'd been in ten years. Teddy would be pissed, but I didn't care.

There's a very strange sense of comfort that comes over you when you take that final step over the point of no return. Somehow you're able to block out the rest of your life and accept the inevitable bad ending looming in front of you. It's like a prize you start to fight for. It's almost romantic. I don't know how else to explain what I was feeling right then. Not happy, not satisfied, just resolved, kind of peaceful.

I felt at home with myself. Scared, terrified, angry . . . but fueled by it.

I turned on the radio and flipped around. Mötley Crüe's "Shout at the Devil" was on the classic rock station. It was so fucking cliché I started laughing and yelling out loud. "I don't fear you! I am not afraid of you!" Crazy Roger at the helm. Enjoy the ride, folks. There's no telling where it'll stop.

My speed accelerated and I topped out at 100 miles per hour.

The southern California night whipped by in broad strokes of royal purple and black, just like the bruises around my eyes. The moon was a silver dagger doing its best to chase me in my rearview mirror. Occasionally I'd check the speedometer and see the face of a madman staring back at me. Nose all busted up, face swollen and flecked with blood, lips split like overcooked hotdogs. I could feel the throbbing, searing pain of that face somewhere distant inside me. That face that wouldn't stop staring back. Could have been me, could have been Skinny Man, could have just been the devil urging me on.

I knew I would see more blood before the night was over. I just hoped it wasn't Victoria's.

A host of other bad metal songs kept tempo for the rest of my drive. Somehow, without knowing it, I'd reached the exit into Rancho Vaiella, and took it so fast I almost scraped along the guardrail.

You're gonna die before you get there.

I slowed down, gripped the wheel a bit looser, and headed out past the polo club. Its green fields flanked both sides of the road, dim white goal posts set off to the sides like dinosaur bones. What did these rich assholes want with Victoria? It couldn't be money for a ransom; they had all the money in the city. White Slave Trade? That shit was just the stuff of myth. Did she owe them money for something?

The road passed under a line of tall palm trees and then meandered past some estates until it reached the one main drag in Rancho Vaiella. It was a pretty short road compared to most main drags in So Cal. A host of restaurants, spas, coffee shops, bakeries, galleries, and real estate offices lined the sides but quickly disappeared as the road made its way up into the hills. Nothing but black trees and fence-lined properties for houses so far up in the hills they couldn't even be seen from the road.

These back streets were like a maze. The people who lived here liked it like that. It gave them a sense of security and privacy, like living in the middle of a labyrinth. I'd been here a couple of times looking for places to paint but had given up since security was tight and the cops would kick you out in a heartbeat for trespassing. There was barely any bit of land here that wasn't privately owned by someone.

I knew the name of the road I was looking for but not exactly how to find it, so I pulled over onto the berm and tried to get my bearing. I was at an intersection, and also at a loss. One other car passed me, slowed to check me out, then kept going. Some dude in a Ferrari.

"Take a picture, buddy."

I drummed my fingers on the steering wheel, feeling time slipping away with each beat.

"Come on, which way, which way?"

I rolled down the window and smelled fresh eucalyptus all around me. It mingled with hints of nearby horse ranches and exhaust from expensive cars. You could call it the smell of money, I guess.

"C'mon, Tooth, if you're still with me . . . they've got your hat."

The moon slipped through the trees and made the street sign on the left reflect back at me. It was as close to any spiritual instruction as I was going to get.

"Thanks, man."

I went left.

●●●

The road wound up further into the hills until I could see the valley of poor man's civilization far below me. What it must be like to live up here every day, looking down on the peasants. No wonder so many of these people gave to charity; they did it out of pity. It made them gods.

I passed a wrought iron gate leading up to an expansive mansion. I might have passed it by and kept searching for more clues except for the fact I could see the front of the house and two police officers at the door talking to a man in a black suit.

I drove past and parked a little ways back on the road, left the keys on the seat, took the gun from beside them, put it down the back of my pants, and walked back to the gate. As I got close I saw a security camera over the top of it. A keypad was built in next to a mailbox on the front the gate. Wasn't gonna get in that way. The wall that ran around the property was not very high, maybe five feet. Certainly low enough to get over. No spikes or broken glass shards set into the top of it either. The odds any cat burglars came up here to rob people were pretty slim. Robbing these people was too much risk. Cops wouldn't think twice about exonerating these homeowners from shooting an intruder.

I walked away from the gate, grabbed the top of the wall and hauled myself up enough to peer over the top. The two cops disappeared inside the house and the front door shut.

"Just two? Not very suspicious, are we?"

Still, I decided to wait. No use getting arrested for trespassing—and whatever else they had already dug up about this night's endeavors—before I had a chance to make sure Victoria was really in there.

It was one of those moments where I wished I smoked. At least it would have killed some time.

As it was I listened to crickets and tried to interpret their language. All I got out of it was meaningless chirping. Not so different from humans, really.

About five minutes later the door opened. I couldn't hear the cops but I could see them shaking hands with the man in the suit, all friendly like. No doubt they were apologizing for the mistake and intrusion. The man in the black suit waved as the cops got back in their car, which was parked up the driveway, and then shut the door. The cruiser backed down the drive, waited for the gate to open, then backed out onto the road not far from where I was hiding behind a tree. They didn't see my car because they weren't looking. As far as they were concerned they'd just been the butt of some bad joke.

I scaled the wall, landed in the yard on the other side, made a split-second decision that would probably get me killed. I ran along the wall to the driveway and sprinted up it in plain sight. The motion lights on the house were still on from the cop car. One camera on the side of the house was covering the long driveway, but I just hoped to hell no one was watching it anymore.

I made it all the way to the car port without incident, stopped to take a breath, and waited to see if anyone came out. Aside from the cars there was no good hiding spot. If someone did come out I was fucked. But as the seconds ticked off and no one came, I considered myself temporarily safe. Guess the monitors weren't watched religiously.

There were two BMWs, a Lexus, a Cadillac SUV, a Porsche, and a Rolls parked side by side in postcard fashion. At the far end was a white SUV, covered in dirt.

Bingo.

I skirted over, grabbed the handle on the side door and pulled it open. The inside was empty. A black rug had been laid on the floor. If there was any blood on it, it probably wouldn't show to the naked eye. Smart.

Not that it mattered. The damn cops hadn't bothered to come back here and check on anything.

I shut the door and slinked around toward the rear yard. Stone statues ringed an inground swimming pool. Off to the left was a covered outdoor seating area with a full kitchen setup and plastic couches. Yard globes illuminated the pathway to the pool, which was itself haloed from soft yellow lights underneath the water. I could see steam coming off the surface. Heated. Nice.

The yard extended downslope to a gardener's shed. As sheds went it was bigger than most one-story houses. It meant nothing to me but for the fact the front door was open a crack. I suddenly had this nagging feeling someone was watching me from inside it.

I drew my gun, cocked it, and sprinted to the outdoor kitchen, wanting to get a closer look. Here, a few yards from the shed, I felt the hairs on my arms stand up. I wasn't sure why. Something just felt wrong.

Victoria is in the house. Hurry up.

No, something's wrong with that shed.
You'll be seen. There are motion sensors everywhere.

That little voice in my head was right. It usually was. I could see the sensors hanging over the windows of the house, mostly angled toward the pool. Apparently they didn't care if anyone stole the lawn furniture in the outdoor kitchen. Probably just didn't want local kids hopping the fence for a free swim. Every kid who lived around here no doubt had their own pool but kids like adventure, and pool hopping has been an American pastime for decades. Those sensors wouldn't register near the shed.

At least I hoped.

Fuck it, I took the chance, and scuttled to the shed as fast as I could, pushed the door open further. Inside was dark. It smelled of cut grass, dirt, wood and residual heat from the day's sun. From the wan light of the lawn's globes I could see a host of landscaping tools. Lawnmowers, weedwackers, chainsaws, pruning shears, saws, bags of fertilizer . . . the kind of place Skinny Man would have a wet dream in.

But all in all pretty typical of a gardening shed. So then why was my Spidey Sense tingling?

"There's nothing here," I whispered. "Wasting time, pal."

But there was something here. I could hear it. A noise that shook me. I realized now I'd heard it from outside. That's why my mind had zeroed in on this place.

Crying.

Someone somewhere was crying. A woman. The low, terrified type of crying one does when one is being held against their will. The same type of crying Jamie did hours before she died.

I spun in a frantic circle, visions of my sister dancing in my wacked-out mind. Visions of a woman with an ax in her head bursting out of Skinny Man's kitchen. Dear God, help me. I do not ever want to hear the sounds of a woman crying again.

"Where the hell is it coming from?"

It seemed to rise like vapor from the ground, entering my body through the soles of my feet and traveling all the way up to my heart. I couldn't tell if it was Victoria or not, but whoever it was they were in trouble.

The cops should be called back, I thought. But I knew the cops would disregard any more calls to this property. I knew whoever was crying was in serious danger and I was the only one who knew they existed.

Dropping to my knees, I put my ear against the metal floor of the shed. The voice was louder now. It was coming from under the floor.

Buried alive? I wondered. *Buried under the shed?*

That made no sense.

My hands felt their way across the floor, looking for some type of hole. What I found was a metal ring, like the kind usually affixed to attic doors. I pulled it and a piece of the floor flipped up a few centimeters before catching on a latch.

The crying wafted out and filled the shed.

It was a trapdoor, locked from underneath.

My heart began to hammer. Sweat sheened my face.

I pulled again in some vain hope I could break the latch, but it wasn't going to come up any more. I tried sliding my fingers in the crack but couldn't even get my pinky in. I wasn't going to get it open without the Jaws of Life.

"No no no no."

I kept my voice low but tried to reassure her. "Victoria? Can you hear me?"

There was no distinct reply, just more crying.

If my gun had a silencer I would have shot the latch, but any report would bring everyone out of the house.

I grabbed a saw off the wall and slid it into the crack, placed the teeth against the metal clip inside. Before I even started to cut I knew it was a ridiculous plan. It would take days to cut through it.

I needed to find a crowbar. *Check the SUV,* I thought.

"Where's Walt?"

I spun, saw Mr. Budweiser in the door of the shed. He had a gun. And it was pointed at me.

Chapter 13

I stood up slowly, raised my arms above my head, gun in one hand, saw in the other, which tapped the ceiling of the shed. The crying still drifted out of the trap door near my feet.

"I said, 'Where's Walt?'"

"Probably in the back of a meat wagon by now."

Mr. Budweiser smiled as he stepped into the dark shed. "Good. He was an asshole anyway. I heard about his stupid grave plan. I knew he should have just killed you but he had to be theatrical."

"Now that's a big word for a man your age. You might want to sit down and take a rest."

"You're funny. But I'm not Walt. I don't play games and I don't banter."

"Technically that was bantering. Just saying."

He was true to his word. He pulled the trigger.

The gun went *click*.

I flinched. Then reacted, lowered my own gun to fire, not caring about noise anymore. But he was on me before I could aim, picked me up in a bear hug and slammed me into the back wall. Teeth and blades from various sharp instruments bit into my back. We hit so hard I lost my breath for the second time tonight and we both bounced off, falling over each other. He tripped over a lawn mower and brought me down on top of him. I almost lost my grip on my gun but caught it by the barrel.

One of his hands clasped around my throat and squeezed. His hands were dry and calloused, as big around as a professional wrestler's. He constricted me like a stress doll, my eyes bulging from my head. I actually felt air puff out of the corners of my eyes. All my oxygen intake was cut off almost immediately. My testicles shriveled into raisins.

I swung the butt of my gun into his face and caught him above the eye, heard something crack around his orbital bone. He roared and loosened his grip for a second and I got about a tablespoon of air back in me. But he ignored his own pain, grunted and huffed as he squeezed my larynx again so tightly I thought he would break my neck.

"Say hi to God for me," he breathed.

"I would," I whispered with my last bit of air, "but I don't think He speaks idiot."

With another roar he lifted me off of him, stood up, and slammed me into another wall. More sharp tools clattered to the floor around us. I flipped the gun around, aimed it at him, but he grabbed my wrist before I could fire and twisted it until I dropped the weapon.

"I'll put 'Funny Bitch' on the shallow grave I bury you in out in the woods."

Spots danced before my eyes. So close, I thought, so close to finding Victoria. And yet I was about to die, no doubt about it. This guy was too big to fight with my bare hands.

He punched me in the stomach for good measure. I had no air in me whatsoever. My head was going fuzzy from oxygen depletion.

As my fists clenched from the pain I realized I was still holding the damn saw. I'd had it the whole damn time. With my last ounce of strength I put it against his leg and zipped it backwards. It cut through his jeans and he pulled his leg back. "Motherfucker!"

It was enough of a surprise for him that he didn't see my other hand go for the gardening shears on the wall beside me. I aimed for his eyes but my world winked out of existence before I could see if I'd struck home.

●●●

I knew I wasn't out long, only a few seconds, because when I woke up Mr. Budweiser was lying on his back next to me, moaning. Still alive. The gardening shears were sticking out of his neck. I hadn't hit his eyes but it was still a good shot.

He was slowly trying to pull them out but, judging by the way he delicately touched the handle, some serious pain was impeding him. He gurgled blood as he swore.

"You motherfucker. You motherfucker. I'm gonna fucking kill

you. I'm gonna . . . ow!"

My body felt lighter now that I had air back in me. Vision was irising like an old movie camera but was good enough for me to get my bearings. My throat was a different story; it throbbed with swelling bruises and when I swallowed it felt like drinking crushed glass. I rolled over onto my stomach and managed to get up on one knee, took a second to acclimate myself to the aching in my body. Mr. Budweiser saw me and did the same.

He came at me on all fours, rose up like a giant praying mantis, like he was gonna hug me and eat my head. "C'mere, you piece of shit. Show you the meaning of pain."

He reached over and picked up my gun. "Gonna kill your ass."

As his arm came up to fire I flat-palmed the gardening shears. Hard.

The tips ripped out the back of his neck with a sound like paper tearing.

He went still. Not dead, just stunned.

I slowly uncurled his fingers from my gun, took it from his hand, and whispered in his ear, "Where's my hat?"

He fell over and his eyes closed. Blood bubbles continued to fizzle out of the wound in his neck for a few seconds, then I felt the spreading pool of blackness on the ground, making my knees wet, and knew he was never going to answer me.

The next minute was spent rubbing my neck and staring at his dying body. Sounds of crying beneath me provided the soundtrack to the scene.

You killed him. You're getting good at that, boy.

I squinted. *Ignore him, Roger.*

When I could move again I searched his body for anything that might open the trapdoor but found nothing. No keys, no miraculous lock cutters that could fit in someone's front pocket. His chest still moved, but it was slowing.

By feeling around the mess for a bit, I found his gun over near the lawn mower. The whole time the sounds of Victoria's crying made me shake.

A quick look back outside showed me the motion lights were still on. Probably from when Mr. Budweiser cut across the lawn. That could be both good or bad. Good if the people in the house knew he was out here; they might ignore the lights going on and off. Bad if they were curious as to what he was doing, in which case they might come out to check.

Again, my test-yourself philosophy cut through: screw it. With both guns, I sprinted back up the lawn, past the outdoor kitchen, back toward the car port. Waited another twenty seconds to see if anyone was coming to investigate, then made for the door on the side of the house near the driveway.

It opened without a sound. Mr. Budweiser had no doubt left it unlocked. Idiot.

I stepped into a dimly-lit entrance hallway lined with old portraits of puritanical-looking men in stiff black suits. They all had white beards and bushy eyebrows, had perfected the serious frown look. The kind of men that burned witches and beat their wives. A few ugly sconces bounced an orange glow off the musty wallpaper, some faded rendition of fleur des lis that reminded me of bad London hotel rooms you see in movies. Lack of windows had managed to trap eons worth of sweat and shoe funk in the walls. The whole place smelled like a gym bag. It was one ugly fucking hallway for such a mansion.

I pulled out the clip from Mr. Budweiser's gun and slid it back home, checked the chamber as well. All seemed in working order. I don't know why it misfired in the shed but I sure as hell wasn't complaining about it. Guns are prone to misfire, it's a common occurrence, or so I've read. That's why your typical gun magazine is laden with trite articles on proper cleaning techniques, about how to keep all the springs and levers well-oiled to avoid snags. A gun misfires once on a police target range, it's removed from use for ever. But your run-of-the-mill perps are pretty lazy, don't want to take the time to keep their tools in working order. Hopefully, if I needed it, it would do better for me.

As silently as I could manage, I slinked down the hallway toward the one door at the end. It pushed open with a slight creak but nothing loud enough to draw attention. I stepped into a pretty large coat room. A collection of gray and brown furs and sleek leather jackets hung from rods along the walls. Hats, gloves and scarves were stacked on shelves above the coats. Some boots lined the floor. A large clock in the shape of a ships helm filled the one empty wall across from the jackets.

Another door was off this room. I pushed it open.

An empty gargantuan kitchen greeted me. The lights were off, but I could see a collection of pots and pans on the counter of the island in the center of the room. Looked like someone was getting ready to make a family dinner then decided against it.

I could also hear music now, flowing out over some kind of in-house speaker system. If I knew more about classical music I might have placed it, but for all intents and purposes it was some kind of chamber music. The kind of crap they play in museums and shit. Me, I prefer guitars, loud drums, and people shouting about how pissed off they are. Complaining about the government or drug control. At least it's something I can identify with.

Above the music and the hum of the refrigerator I heard distant voices. Somewhere in the house people were conversing. Not for the first time since arriving I wondered if these homeowners were gun happy, and if so, how close they kept their pieces to them. If I got out of this alive I was gonna buy a bulletproof vest to match my gun.

I inched past the center island toward another hallway running off the kitchen that led deeper into the house. I could see all the way to the end of it, to an area that looked like a sitting room. In eyesight was a gaudy recliner and a china cabinet displaying a collection of porcelain dolls. They each probably cost more than my yearly rent. I took my steps as slowly as possible, listening for any betrayal from the floorboards. There was quite a bit of squeaking, which was to be expected considering how old this house was, but the music and party chatter seemed to drown out my approach.

When I reached the end I stopped and leaned against the wall, trying in vain to make out the conversation coming from a few rooms away.

"Do you remember that girl from Holland?" A man's voice. Distinguished, older perhaps.

"Of course." A woman answering. Definitely older judging from her rasp. "Such a pleasant evening all around. Wish we could have invited Joseph over for that one. Has anyone heard from him lately. We do miss his anecdotes."

"He will just have to come another time."

"The man is intolerable." A third voice, also male. "I see no reason to converse with him any longer. Let him do his thing on his stubborn sailing trip and get himself lost in the Bermuda Triangle, I say. Save us all the trouble of having to hear his ridiculous hunting stories."

"Yes, well, Joseph aside, that girl from Holland was quite a treat. Dare say we won't find another like her in some time."

There was a collection of here-here's from numerous other people, accompanied by the clinking of crystal. Dinner party at a kidnapper's house. How quaint.

I peeked into the sitting room, saw it was empty and slinked through it, found yet another hallway lined with portraits and old photographs, and followed it closer to the voices. As I moved the chamber music seemed to move with me. At least six other hallways broke off of this one, each dimly lit with iron sconces and small electric chandeliers. At the ends of them were more vast rooms filled with couches and chairs, the occasional desk and bookshelf. Giant windows looked out into the back- and side yards. I stayed my course toward the voices, vaguely aware that the air in the house was growing warmer. The conversation, however, remained bland.

"Markus Fritch bought a villa in Tuscany . . ."

". . . which is the only reason the market sustains in this day and age . . ."

". . . Fritch was just about forced out of Rio . . ."

". . . fabulous vintage that has been put up for auction from Sothebys at a mere ten thousand per bottle . . ."

". . . says Veles, and I believe there will be penance to pay . . ."

". . . I hope dinner is served soon. I'm starving and the kids are with the nanny tonight but I know she drinks and falls asleep early . . ."

". . . that new novel by Harrison Lucas, about the Polish cargo trains during the war . . ."

". . . I believe it was during Cologne. I was flying for Operation Millennium and I had met this pretty little nurse . . ."

". . . My doctor says the cancer has disappeared, which I told him it would. Of course I'd explain my therapy to him but he would not be enlightened, I should think."

". . . I believe that was 1933. I remember my mother working at the rubber factory . . ."

". . . bought into the computer stocks, but I am regrettably second guessing myself now . . ."

I passed through a small study and into another of this labyrinth's hallways, was almost at the end of it when a giant ink blot of a shadow fell on the wall next to me. Somebody coming my way from the party. I grabbed the nearest door and opened it, saw it was a closet, and ducked inside. The smell of the ocean greeted me, but I realized it was just some kind of detergent on all the linens inside. Owing to the age of the house the door had an old keyhole at waist height, through which light spilled onto my jeans. I knelt down and watched like some peeping Tom as a very large man with muscles bigger than washing machines walked by holding what looked like a machine gun he'd ripped off a tank.

Correction: two men. Another man came into sight, pulling up the rear. He had also been visited by the guns and ammo fairy. This piece was smaller, some kind of hybrid Uzi, but no less intimidating.

I already knew I wasn't in Kansas anymore but I wasn't expecting the munchkins to be packing such serious heat. The tiny gun in my hand felt useless in comparison.

The men disappeared around the end of the hallway, went to wherever hulking security sociopaths go. I waited a few seconds for good measure then let myself out of the closet and resumed my investigation, making note of any possible hiding spaces along the way, praying that the bulletproof vest I needed so badly would materialize out of thin air for me. I glanced back every five seconds to make sure the Heavy Artillery Twins weren't doubling back.

Finally, the room with the gathering came into view. I squatted behind a chaise lounge a room away and assessed the crowd.

There's a unique excitement that comes with spying, especially after you've just shoved gardening shears into a man's throat and then broken into a rich asshole's house. It's the kind of feeling that makes you feel braver. Like you are privy to a universal secret. And perhaps more, that you can control its outcome. Example: I could wait until one of these jerks went to the bathroom, follow, and reduce the party's number by one. I could run out guns blazing. I could lock them all in and set fire to the house. When people don't know you're watching, you realize how vulnerable they are. These are the feelings that always scare me. Probably because I'm always where I shouldn't be, in a situation that scrambles my brain.

We'll have to put it all in my file later.

Moving on.

About twelve guests in all, each formally dressed, the youngest of which was easily pushing fifty years old. They were drinking wine and hobnobbing with one another like they'd been farm raised to attend State dinners. All in all, pretty standard fare for your average old money crowd. If you've ever seen any ancient black and white film about southern landowners you know the type of scene I'm referring to here. Save for the one little issue of the terrified girl crying in some underground bunker.

In the center of the room a large dining table had been prepared with good china and centerpieces that would make Martha Stewart proud. A fire crackled in a grand marble fireplace, over which sat some gaudy sculptures on the mantle. Why they needed a fire in summer was beyond me; probably just to show off the fireplace itself. The ceiling extended upwards two stories to a large crystal chandelier that threw tiny rainbows onto the crown molding. I could just make out a landing running around the second floor up there, bookshelves against the walls, all overlooking the table.

I could also make out another two goons at the far end of the room, each with a machine gun slung over their shoulders. The larger one looked like he should have Princess Leia chained to him.

No one in the party seemed to care much about the incredibly dangerous weaponry around them. If any of those goons accidentally slipped a finger against a trigger these guests would be shredded like soft cheese. I'd have scratched my head out of confusion at the stupidity of it all if I wasn't so scared to make a move.

The scene continued to play out in monotony for a few more seconds until a man with a bushy white mustache put his hands in the air in a universal gesture of attention. The guests all hushed. For some reason I did, too.

"Thank you, thank you. I hope you're all having a good time. And once again I'm honored to be hosting tonight's soirée. Maryellen and I just had the Observation Room on the third floor redone and we're eager to show it to you all a little later." He put his arm around the woman next to him to punctuate the point. No doubt it was Maryellen, his wife. Even from my hiding spot I could see her wedding ring was so big it would take an X-Wing squadron to destroy it.

"The room is exquisite," she said. "You can see clear to Rosanna Canyon. It's quite beautiful."

"Take my wife's word on it."

"It's a lovely home, Marshall." A voice from somewhere out of sight.

The mustached man ignored the compliment, continued: "I just want you to know that I appreciate you all coming. You all look fantastic, as usual. I wish we got together more often these days, but I certainly cherish any time we can find to dine together. Perhaps we will find ways to meet more often in the future. I know we all look forward to these dinners with such fervor. Which brings me to my next point. Dinner will be served in a couple of minutes so I suggest we all sit and get comfortable. I can see you are enjoying my choice of vintages so I'm also having more wine brought out—"

I didn't hear what he said next because I heard new voices from behind me. Glancing back, I could see the shadows of people coming toward me from where the first two goons had gone.

Without thinking, I scurried around the chaise lounge and hooked a right around the nearest corner into a tiny sitting room. Stairs to my left ascended to the second floor. I took them as fast and as silently as I could just as two bodies passed by the chaise lounge and walked toward the dining room. I couldn't see who it was but had to assume it was the gunmen; the floor kind of shook as they walked.

At the top of the stairs I found myself in a small guest bedroom. The light was off, the bedding untouched. The ugliest painting of some sword-wielding dancing wolf creatures met my eye. It was uglier than a two-headed camel fucking a rocking chair; must have cost a fortune. A second door was open to the landing with the bookshelves running around the dining room below. The sounds of chairs being pushed in and out, and glasses being refilled, rose up and bounced off the high ceiling. I lay on my belly and slithered like a snake toward the base of the railing, peeked down at the guests below.

The two goons had indeed returned.

They were carrying something.

A naked woman. Maybe in her twenties. She looked dead, eyes closed, body limp. Taut skin and elfish face. A real sexy girl.

It wasn't Victoria. I had no idea who it was. The girl who I'd heard crying?

Goons three and four quickly removed all the centerpieces and withdrew the flowing white table cloth, revealing a double wide stainless steel operating table ringed with a thin collecting basin. On the table were four metal shackles.

They laid the naked girl on the table and fastened her wrists and ankles into the shackles.

Ice flows of sweat broke out on the back of my neck and cut glacial ravines down to the balls of my feet.

The dinner guests oohed and ahhed as the girl was locked in place. They raised their knives and forks and grinned.

I shook a little. I saw Jamie's face float through my mind.

"Wait for it." The mustached man held up a palm. "The drug should be wearing off any . . . . Ah, here she comes."

The girl slowly opened her eyes.

Chapter 14

She barely had time to ascertain her surroundings before the nightmare began. An old woman with a beehive of silver hair shoved her steak knife into the girl's thigh and sliced open a deep gouge that severed an artery. With the knife she flipped out the artery and let it dangle like a long blue worm. Then she cut through the flesh straight to the bone, ignored the arc of blood that Pollocked her face. The other dinner guests followed suit and sliced into the young girl with a zeal I had only seen before on Discovery Channel documentaries about starving animals in the Serengeti. The young girl's tight skin parted in long red slices as the blades ran fissures down her body. Streams of blood zig-zagged down her sides and pooled on the cold metal table, shimmering like mercury. A grinning man reached into one of the long slices on the girl's bicep, grabbed each side of the cut, and ripped it open like he was looking inside a goody bag. Bone and muscle shredded apart under his fingers. He tore out a long strip of striated muscle and stared at it in awe.

"Ah, but I forgot the toast!" The mustached man again. "How gauche of me."

"But she looks so good and we're hungry," chuckled the old white-haired bitch. "Make it a fast one, Marshall."

The drugs on the girl must still have been dissipating because she wasn't crying or screaming yet. But she managed a murmur and started trying to pull her arms and legs free, pumping more arterial blood onto her white flesh and the table beneath her. She was able to raise her head a little and look in horror at the deep red ravines cut across her belly, breasts, legs and ribs. One of the gun-toting apes, a fifth one I hadn't seen before, came a little closer to the table, watching her intently.

Marshall put a hand on the man's barreled chest. "She's not going anywhere, Ben, let her be."

The goon backed off. I slowly put my guns through the railing and aimed at Ben. I could shoot him, I was sure of it. Even with my somewhat blurred vision from my busted nose, I could take his head clean off from here. But the other four hulks would have a bead on me in a second, and with those weapons would shred me into geek pasta. So I just kept watching and shaking.

Marshall raised his glass of wine. "To good friends, good health, a banner year for the market, and of course, the flesh of our salvation."

"Praise Veles," they chanted.

"And now, everybody, let's dig in."

"Here here," the guests replied, sipping their wine.

Marshall glanced down at the young girl, smiled with old yellow teeth.

She was crying now. She was becoming lucid. She was scared out of her fucking mind.

So was I.

"Hello, my dear," Marshall said to her. "Thanks for coming to dinner." He thrust his head down and clamped his teeth on her nose, crunching the cartilage and thrashing his jaw back and forth, and came away with the nose in his mouth. He chewed it like steak gristle and swallowed it all in one gulp. Beneath the gory hole in her face, her mouth was open in some attempt to scream. But no sound came out. The pain was too intense. Then, Marshall picked up his steak knife, and with a demonic grin, drove it down into her belly and began sawing at her.

This time she did scream, high-pitched and laced with gurgles. The shriek resonated inside the core of my soul.

Ben stepped a bit closer, finger on his trigger, watching her intently, but ignoring the massacre.

Her screams did not deter the dinner guests from following Marshall's lead, and they stabbed their knives into her with great glee, laughing and kibitzing as they cut chunks of her flesh away, picked it up on their forks, and put it in their mouths.

They chewed her flesh with the savagery of a pride of hungry lions. Her blood ran down their chins and they merely wiped it back into their mouths with their fingers. A bald man with black-rimmed glasses grabbed a ribbon of flayed flesh and pulled it all the way down the middle of her chest, like a giant hangnail, yanking it loose and sucking it into his mouth like it was spaghetti.

Her screams transcended anything human.

Another woman gingerly cut the girl's stomach out, careful to keep it intact, and then opened its contents in front of her, picking out blobs and chunks of black and red goo that she sucked on and devoured.

I wanted to shoot them all, but now all four guards lifted their guns as if they suddenly sensed something was wrong. Or maybe they were just tense from the screams.

Save her, Roger. Save her!

I can't! I'll get shot!

I wanted so badly to close my eyes, but I just couldn't. I was frozen in shock and horror, watching them eat this poor girl alive.

An elderly woman went for the girl's face. Took her fork and stabbed it into the girl's lower lip, pulled it back, sawing at the pink puffy skin with her knife until it ripped off. She swallowed it in a single gulp like it was a piece of shrimp.

Marshall jammed his fork into her left eye socket, scooped the eye out, snapped the veins holding it in her head, took it off the tines with his fingers and ate it like a cherry plucked from a Manhattan. Pink goo dribbled down his chin and the woman next to him, his wife, leaned over and licked the juice off of him and *mm-mmm*ed as she swallowed it.

It went on and on for what seemed an eternity. They cut every bit off flesh from her body and wolfed it down. When her ribs were exposed they gave up on utensils and hooked their fingers into the bones, pulling with all their might until her ribcage tore loose from her body.

Eventually, she stopped screaming. She wasn't even dead at this point. Her body still twitched and shook. She'd gone into shock and shut down. Which was just as well, because it was a happier place for her to be. It made me feel a little better about not doing anything. But hardly. I felt the same way I'd felt watching that strange lady burn to death in Skinnyman's basement, after he'd wedged an ax in her skull. I just wished for her to die so it would end, so I wouldn't bear the guilt of inactivity any longer.

"Who's turn is it tonight?" someone asked around a mouthful

of the girl's flesh.

"I do believe Helen has the honors tonight," Marshall said.

"Lucky," said someone at the end of the table who was sucking on a small white finger bone.

And with that Marshall reached into the gaping hole that had been the girl's chest and cut loose her heart. He handed it to an impish woman across the table whose once-green dress was now black with thick blood and peppered with small chunks of meaty gristle. She said thank you and sawed a wedge free from the heart, letting the blood collect in the basin before her. With a theatrical curtsy she began eating it. He eyes rolled back in her head, intoxicated by the taste. The young girl's bowels evacuated, a clear indication she had finally succumbed. This didn't seem to make a difference to the maniacs eating her. They made no move to wipe it away. I could smell the new scent of feces up at my height. Maybe these psychos thought it was just part of the delicacy.

Someone to Marshall's left produced a small hammer and smashed it into the girl's head. *Crack! Crack! Crack!* Until he'd split open her skull, at which point he drove his fork inside and started pulling out bits of her pink brain. He passed the pieces around the table so everyone could eat some.

At this point I realized I was crying, realized I was squeezing the guns so tightly I might shatter them like eggshells. Who had she been and what had she done to deserve this? More to the point, who the fucking hell were these sick fucks?

The dinner guests leaned back in their chairs, their clothes dotted with blood and their faces and hands stained a deep maroon. A few of them got about picking the meat out of their teeth while others merely rubbed their full bellies. Some old fat guy at the far end was sucking on a rib bone, getting every last bit of meat off of it.

The girl on the table was nothing but a ravaged cadaver, pink bones and torn meat, slick with red goo. Her face was a giant hole. Her intestines were roped out across her thighs . . . or what had been her thighs. Her jaw was exposed through tattered cheeks. Both her eyes were dissolving in the bellies of these beasts.

I slowly rolled over and stared up at the chandelier, saw the etchings in the base. Pictures. Something that looked like hieroglyphics from Mars. Maybe they were supposed to be angels, or maybe demons, or maybe demigods from another realm. It looked like they were wolves with six arms dancing and waving swords. Kind of like the painting in the bedroom. None of it mattered but I couldn't stop staring, not really seeing it to be honest, but rather watching the images of that girl being eaten alive roll through my brain like seaweed on a massive Pacific swell.

Red Tide. The smell of brine and blood. Something more than murder happening beneath me. Pictures of multi-armed wolves and blood rituals and human cannibalistic orgies.

Get a grip, Roger. Get to Victoria, find her and get her out of here.

Beneath me I heard our host's voice yet again. "I trust everyone is sated? Does anyone need more wine?"

A collection of grunts and burps. Etiquette was apparently selective at this point. A man's voice, deep and lethargic. "To wit, Marshall, I can't eat another bite. Fantastic find, though, I must say. Perfectly sweet and tender. I feel her youth in me already. Veles will be pleased."

"Yes, wherever did you find her?" This from that beehived witch. "There was so little fat that my jaw barely aches."

"I have my methods," Marshall responded. "I have some feelers out in the community, good friends, people who know how to find things. Now don't look at me like that. There has been no disclosure as to our meeting, and the terms were made perfectly clear to these hired hands. They are men who ask no questions except when they will be paid, which they are upon delivery."

"But I saw a man here earlier . . . . He looked distrustful to say the least. All those tattoos. And did I hear that the police came by?"

"The police were here for a minute on a prank call. They are long gone. Not the first time the police have poked about, you know that. And I repeat, my help ask no questions and take their pay. Trust me, Belle. They're petty thieves that would be laughed out of any courtroom. Isn't that right, Judge?"

The same deep lethargic voice from before: "Oh yes, it's pure nonsense to believe less. Let anyone in this room stand in the legal arena against said riffraff I've seen Marshall employ. The outcome is assured in our favor. Still, Marshall, we must be careful."

"I am always careful. And to show you how much I have been careful and how much I have been anticipating tonight's events, I have a surprise for you all."

There was mass bleating from the table as everyone tried to guess what the surprise could be. Curious, I rolled over and resumed my bird's eye view on the whackadoo party. I tried hard not to stare at the decimated corpse on the medical table, its arms and legs still bound in cuffs, but it was a beacon to my eye. It would be a beacon to a blind man's eye. I could see straight through to her spine.

Marshall raised his hands again, quieted everyone down. He was good at that; the response he got was almost Pavlovian. "As you know it's been six months since our last meeting. Greta was supposed to host last time but alas was taken from us before her time. Lucky her. She was called upon to serve."

There was a collective reply: "Praise Veles."

"Praise him," Marshall said. He coughed and resumed. "Which means, we have been without for an extra three months. Our great lord has been weakened by our brief reprieve."

"It did give us time to finish the Observation Room," said Marshall's wife, Maryellen. I saw her teeth were still stained red, as were her lips. There was a splotch of blood near her ear.

Behind her, Ben the Lovable Security Guard showed the slightest hint of a smile. I wondered why he and the rest of the gunmen weren't eating, but decided not to dwell on it too hard. He didn't look like a cannibal, didn't have the glassy-eyed stares of the rest of the dinner party, but he sure as hell looked like he wanted nothing more than to rip someone's head off of their shoulders. I'm sure death was no big deal to him. Pretty sure he was getting off on the whole thing.

"It did indeed," Marshall replied to his wife. "But more to the point, it gave me ample time to plan this party and so I have arranged for a special dessert for everyone tonight."

"Oh, Marshall, I can't eat another bite," said the judge. He rubbed his rotund belly to illustrate his point. I thought about shooting him in the gut, spilling his insides onto the table in front of him, hoping his friends would eat him.

I let the thought drift away.

"I will blow up if I ingest anything beyond air," said Belle the Beehive. "Much as I enjoyed the meal, a lady must behave as such."

Marshall picked up a bottle of wine, held it to his nose. "We're all friends here, Belle, do not fret about such nonsense. I will be bringing dessert out in a little bit. Consider it my gift to you all for making the long drive out here. Eat what you can, the rest can be taken home. It is for Veles we unbuckle our belts this night. We must make him proud."

Some of the guests giggled, some rolled their eyes the way your friends might at a bar when someone orders an extra round no one really wants. Still, I could tell they were gonna eat whatever it was. And whatever it was, I was sure, was going to be alive.

Victoria.

I slithered back toward the spare bedroom, listening to Marshall's upbeat words as he poured himself more wine.

"I suggest we retire to the Observation Room and I will have brandy and port served. Donald, you are a port fan, if I remember. As I mentioned, we have had the room remodeled so dessert will be served there in a little bit. I propose we digest what we can and let our stomachs settle in the meantime. Judge, you will love the new telescope we purchased. The stars are divine. Now, if everyone would follow me, the night is still young."

Chapter 15

From inside the bedroom I heard the guests leaving the dining room, making their way past the chaise lounge and down another hall. I waited a minute longer until I heard their voices drift up to the same level of the house as me, and then continued up another level.

For the sake of caution I peered back around the doorjamb and down at the girl on the table. Two goons remained, watching like bored children at church while two other men in rubber uniforms, each carrying a small surgical saw, unlatched the body, cut off the hands and feet, and placed everything in a large plastic cocoon-like sac, the kind you fed into a large furnace or buried way out at sea somewhere.

They carried the limp plastic case from the room and disappeared, leaving the two gunmen alone to make friends with each other. But they didn't even bother to glance at one another let alone talk. To see their tight jaws and stone cold eyes you'd think they were under some kind of spell. I'd read my fair share of comics with villains who used hypnosis on people, but always felt it was a cheesy and outdated plot device. But now I wasn't so sure. These guys looked like they'd walk off a cliff if you commanded it. Still, I recalled the way Ben had stepped to the table to silence the girl when she was waking up. They clearly still moved of their own accord to some degree. If only I had silencers on my weapons, I would have done the world a favor right then and there.

Instead, I made my way back down the stairs, into the small sitting room, looked around for a sense of sanity. More portraits here just like the ones I'd seen before—old men with mutton chops and high collars, black and white photos of some families that looked like they'd been created in mad science experiments. And two paintings that showed more dancing wolves with swords, only this time they were all staring up at some orange man with one eye. The word PSOGLAV was painted in what resembled a blood stain at the bottom. I had no idea what it meant.

Next to this was one of my own paintings. I wanted to tear it down and strangle Marshall with it. I wanted to slash it and burn it and take back the notion I'd made money off this lunatic.

You want to feel his blood run down your arms, Roger. You want to crack his ribs and spill his life onto the street.

Skinny Man again. He'd been silent for a bit but was back.

"Let it rest, asshole. I already told you you're not real."

Real enough for you. You're the one arguing with me. Hey, did I ever tell you about the time I chewed your sister's cunt in half?

The gun came up so quick and smashed into my head I didn't even realize I did it. My busted nose sang out behind my eyes. The pain cut through me and cleared away the voice, allowed me to focus once again.

"Ow."

A small hallway ran off the back wall. It must run almost parallel to the larger hallway the guests had gone down. That it was skinnier than usual made me think it was perhaps a separate hallway for the staff, and if so, that could make moving down it a pretty stupid choice. All the staff seemed to be armed for war or ready to butcher someone. But, fuck it.

As I snuck down it, trying my best to be quiet, I weighed the options of either going back to the shed and just shooting the fucking chain on the trap door, or finding an inside access to whatever subterranean rooms this place held. I opted for plan two, remembering I was still contending with machine guns and cannibals.

The walls in this tight hallway smelled off, like they were covering something fetid. There was a nice collection of mold around the baseboards. I almost screamed as I passed by a small mirror and saw my reflection, not realizing it was me but thinking it was a goon trying to surprise me. The doctors were going to have a hard time putting my nostrils back in place.

Deeper now, I could no longer hear the Donner Party's conversation two stories up. But I wasn't too concerned with that. I was more concerned about what would happen if I didn't find Victoria before the rubber men or Ben went to get her. The hallway turned left and passed by two closed doors. Staff quarters, perhaps. I stopped briefly outside them both and listened, but heard nothing from the other sides.

This hallway ended at yet another kitchen, this one dirtier and rank with some kind of vinegar stench. The lights were off but an orange nightlight over the sink threw coffee stains of wan light against the walls. A collection of knives and cleavers lay on the counter near some cutting boards, all stained brown. In the dim light it could easily have been blood. More shivers raced down my back. It reminded me of Skinny Man's basement, the way he had left out his carving implements for us to stare at. The way he'd managed to get inside our heads when he wasn't even in the room with us. You know, it's your own imagination that is your worst enemy.

Only in that instance Skinny Man had lived up to everything my own brain could devise.

And then some.

"Could just be porkchops, dude." My whisper of hope didn't work. Even if it was just beef or pork blood, it didn't change the fact a girl had just been eaten alive tonight. It didn't change the fact I was in some bloodthirsty Twilight Zone.

Two doors were on opposite walls here. I tried the one to my left, opened it slowly with my guns pointed ahead of me. Inside was a small pantry, shelves stocked with canned goods and large bags of flour and rice. A chunk of dried meat hung from a rope at the back. Could have been a smoked ham, could have been a woman's thigh. What looked like a butcher's stamp of quality could just as easily have been a tattoo.

Shut the door and move on. Don't think about it.

I opened the other door, found myself standing at the top of a set of wooden stairs that descended into blackness.

The cellar.

Actually, I should capitalize that—The Cellar—because with a mansion this big the basement was bound to go on forever.

I felt around the inside wall for a light switch but couldn't find one. My hand brushed through the soft wisps of cobwebs and nothing else. Didn't see a switch or bulb anywhere on the wall near the door in the kitchen either.

Down into the darkness, buddy. You've done it before.

I took a step, heard the stair groan. Took another, felt the air get just a bit colder. I kept going like this, steady and cautious, guns in front of me. A mustiness tickled my nose. Shadows engulfed me as I continued; the air became heavier. When I reached the bottom, I waited for my eyes to adjust, relying on what little light crawled down after me from the kitchen nightlight. It took a few seconds before I could ascertain my position. There was an enormous cavern to my right: the underneath of the mansion. I walked carefully into the darkness, slowly making out stone walls and wooden doors and old furniture covered in sheets and tarps. A freestanding mirror threw my image back at me and gave me the heebie-jeebies. I was beginning to hate mirrors big time.

Another twenty paces and the light from upstairs was no longer able to penetrate the darkness. To say I was scared and tense is an understatement. I had no way of knowing if anyone else was down here with me. I didn't even know what direction I was shuffling in. Would I knock something over and attract the Goons? Would I suddenly feel an arm around my neck as someone attacked me?

Was that breathing I heard?

Yep, but just my own.

Maybe you'll run into your friend, Tooth's, corpse.

Figures Skinny Man would pop up when I couldn't see where I was going. "I'm gonna figure out a way to get to Hell so I can kill you again."

Looking forward to it.

As I moved my ears were able to guess the size of the room. Hard to explain, but if you ever go into a ballroom and close your eyes, you'll know what I mean. You can just tell the place is huge.

Then I heard it. A whimper. Far away, but definitely human. A girl's voice. I stood still listening, trying to figure out where it was coming from. It seemed to just drift around my head and play with my inner ear. It was incredibly faint; if I'd been breathing any harder I wouldn't have heard it.

It stopped for a few seconds then picked up again, and this time I was able to follow it off to my left. I let it pull me forward like I was under a spell. My shin banged into something hard and wooden and I grit my teeth but managed to keep from yelping.

Eventually I came to a wall. More paintings leaned against it. I could see them because a thin ribbon of dim yellow light fell on my shoes, betraying the outline of a door right in front of me. If the light on the other side had been out I would never have found it. I pulled it open and smelled dirt. Not dirt as in someplace messy, but actual dirt.

Earth.

It was a tunnel, like a mineshaft. Dirt floor and walls, with rickety-looking crossbeams providing support. A sallow yellow bulb hung from a cable about twenty yards down. It flickered and buzzed.

In times like this you swallow inadvertently just to find out you still have spit. I didn't have any, because all my body's moisture was sweating out of my palms.

Homes should not have dirt tunnels under them. Homes should not have paintings of wolf creatures and medical tables for strapping down live people either.

The girl's timid crying came from the opposite end of the tunnel. I knew it was Victoria, I could just tell. I'd longed for so long to kiss her that I knew every sound her voice could make. Knew what she sounded like yawning, stretching, laughing, sneezing.

This tunnel obviously went under the back lawn to the room beneath the shed, but that knowledge didn't make me move any faster. I was still just trying to wrap my head around all of this.

Just as well, Roger. You never save the girl first. You didn't save that poor bitch upstairs.

That was enough of a guilty push to get me moving. I stepped slowly, watching out for booby traps, once touching the dirt wall to see how sturdy this tunnel was. The dirt broke away in clumps and cascaded to the ground. Shit, the whole thing would probably collapse if I farted too loud. I followed the tunnel until I reached yet another door. Victoria's cries were plain as day on the other side. A man's voice was talking, laughing, having a conversation with someone. I couldn't make out the words, but I could tell he was tormenting Victoria.

Slowly, I turned the doorknob, opened the door. These people really should invest in locks, but I certainly wasn't going to complain. I slithered around the door into a dark wooden room lit orange with low bulbs. It reminded me of a sauna, was as hot as one too. Only instead of a fire pit in the middle, there was an empty chair.

Ringing the room were large cages, like the kind you transport circus animals in. Big animals. All the cages were stained with blood. A corpse, skeletal and rotted, lay in a fetal position in the cage to my left. The others were empty.

Except for the one directly in front of me.

Victoria was curled up in it, her hair over her face. She was naked. Her body shook as she whimpered.

I wanted to run to her but something didn't feel right.

The male voice. Where was it now? There was no one else in here.

I stepped into the center of the room, swung my gun around, focused for a second on the corpse but did my best to ignore it.

Whoever had been in here was now gone. To where?

I saw a second door between two of the cages. This place was just one creepy set of rooms after another. Whoever had been here must have left just as I came in, which either meant he'd heard me or I was just one lucky son of a bitch. But with my luck, it was probably the former.

"Victoria." I moved to her cage and examined the lock. It needed some kind of big ass key, but I figured a bullet would work just as well. I'd been holding off on firing any rounds to avoid detection but I wasn't about to play find-the-key at this point. There was an exit up to the shed somewhere nearby, had to be. Probably a ladder. We could be out of here in thirty seconds if we hurried.

Before I could think any harder about it, I shut the door to the tunnel, came back and told Victoria to move to the other side of the cage. She didn't move, didn't even acknowledge that she'd heard me. She just kept whimpering, curling into herself like a beaten animal.

For all I knew she was in shock and thought I was one of the lunatics who'd been abusing her.

"Victoria, I'm gonna shoot the lock. Just . . . just don't move then, okay? And don't scream. Please."

I aimed at a funky angle, hoping the bullet would either lodge in the lock or career off in a safe direction, and squeezed the trigger.

Bang!

The shot was cacophonous. God knows where the bullet went but I felt fine and I didn't see Victoria get hit.

The cage door swung open with a hard yank. "Victoria, it's me, Roger." I raced in and put my arms around her. "Please be okay."

Suddenly she screamed and tried to burrow through the floor between the bars. I shook her a bit and pulled her close, feeling her naked body against me. I'd wanted to feel her skin against mine for so long, but not like this. Not after what she'd suffered.

"Victoria, look at me. Please. It's me, it's Roger."

Gently, I lifted her head and brushed the hair from her eyes. Her face was a puffy pink mess, slick with tears and snot. She trembled as she met my eyes, slowly realizing she knew me from somewhere. Must be the broken nose throwing her off. But she seemed to be getting it.

"See? It's me. Roger. We need to get out of here, okay. I need you to move."

Again, she didn't say anything, but she didn't break eye contact. And then slowly, like a timid creature, she reached up and touched my face.

When she did this I saw her bare breasts, and again I felt ashamed for seeing her in this state. It was all wrong, and I felt something special had been taken from me. I know that's selfish, but I still felt it.

"Can you walk?" I asked. "They're coming back down soon. We can't stay here. My car is outside. We just have to get out."

"Roger." She mumbled my name, just about slurred it.

Shit, she'd been drugged. Her pupils were dilated. She probably couldn't walk.

"I hurt," she managed. "Stuck . . . needle . . . in me . . ."

"I know. I'm sorry. I'm so sorry."

"Hurt me inside. My insides . . ."

"I know. I killed them. And now I'm gonna get you outta here."

"Gabe? Need Gabe."

Can't say that her asking for her fiancé didn't make me feel a bit depressed, but I didn't know if it was because I was still jealous or because I felt terrible having to tell her the truth. I was afraid that if she went into further shock she would just lie down and die right here. Poor girl didn't deserve this. No one did. Then again, if

I lied she would worry about it instead of focusing on getting out.
I chose my poison: "He's dead. It was fast."

Her mouth trembled. "No." She closed her eyes.

"I killed the guy that did it."

"No." Her mouth pulled back in a giant sob. Her chest heaved
with gasps of anguish and she began to shake. It was obvious she'd
been hoping to reunite with Gabe. Maybe it had helped her get
through this ordeal so far, as much as she was still sane.

"I'm sorry, Victoria. He died trying to save you. Please don't let
it be in vain. We have to go."

Stupid movie lines, but somehow it got her up. Well, not exactly up, but she used my body to start to rise. I slipped my arms
under her and lifted her the rest of the way. As we rose I saw giant
teeth marks on her back from where Mr. Budweiser had chewed at
her during his savagery. I also happened to catch a glimpse of the
area between her legs, which was now blue and swollen.

She was going to have trouble walking no matter what.

I haphazardly took off my *Ghost in the* Shell shirt and fumbled
it over her head. It didn't cover her bottom, but I just hoped it made
her feel a little more protected. Normally I wouldn't want to show
my lily-white body to girls until after several dates, but it was a sac-
rifice I could live with. I'm not really muscular, just a bit wiry. Did-
n't matter, she didn't notice. But she tugged the shirt down absently,
happy for whatever cover she could get.

"This way." I helped her limp toward the strange door between
the cages, once again noticing the knotted-up corpse and doing my
best to look away. A tiny window set at head level in the door let me
see another dirt tunnel on the other side. It was dark, and only the
light from this strange human zoo room provided any light. But
sure enough, I could see the outline of what looked like a ladder up
ahead. I figured it led up to the shed.

Bingo. Freedom.

When I pulled at the door it wouldn't open. I knew that was a
bad sign right away. The guy who left must have locked it. Sure as
shit they knew I was here now. "They brought you down that way,
huh? Down the ladder?" I was sort of just making conversation, to
keep Victoria focused, but was equally as curious why they hadn't
taken her through the house and cellar. Probably to hide her from

the guests. To keep her as far from the road as possible.

To keep her a secret little present until dessert time.

My guess, the door under the shed was also reserved as some kind of escape route. Whoever was down here must have gone up and out. Probably alerting Ben and his gun goons even now.

The time of silence and secrecy was over. I backed us up, aimed my Glock and fired. The lock splintered and the door opened a sliver on its own. The scent of fresh dirt swam through the opening and reminded me how close to being buried alive we were. "Just to the ladder and we're free. Ready?"

She nodded, shifted her arm over my shoulder to walk better. I glanced down to make sure she was moving her legs, saw her bruised genitalia again and felt ashamed for staring, but I wanted to make sure she wouldn't stumble, wanted to make sure whatever drug they'd given her wasn't impeding her mobility. Basically I didn't want to have to carry her.

"That's good. Almost there."

"Roger."

"What?" I was still looking down. She was doing good. She was going to get through this.

"No."

"No what?"

"Please stop."

"huh?"

"Stop. Just . . . stop."

"What?"

"I see him." She started to shake so badly I almost dropped her.

"Who?" I looked up and watched a big man in a Red Sox hat step out of the shadows just beyond the ladder. Sonofabitch had just been waiting for me, knowing I would come this way.

"No. No more," Victoria cried. I was leading her right into the path of the man who had last raped her.

Right into Bob

Chapter 16

He genuinely looked a little shocked. "You?"

"Me."

I raised my guns, took aim, but he ducked into some kind of alcove next to the ladder and disappeared before I could fire. His arm came around fast and squeezed off a shot from his own gun. The bullet echoed in the tunnel and struck the dirt wall a few feet in front of us. Bits of dirt stung my face.

"Shit!" I threw both myself and Victoria to the ground, and scrambled back inside the cage room, dragging her as fast as I could. Another bullet hit the door above our heads just as we leapt to the side.

Victoria was crying, holding her knees to her chest. "No more no more no more."

She was starting to lose it and I needed her to be lucid if I was going to get us out of here.

I pointed to the tunnel door leading back to the basement. "Go that way. Get into the shadows and hide."

"I can't. I can't move."

"Yes, you can."

"I can't feel my legs."

Crap, I'd forgotten about the drugs. She must only be able to walk with my help. "You've got to try. Crawl if you have to, okay?"

I peeked around the door, saw Bob peering out of the alcove at me in a weird type of mirrored movement. We both fired at the same time. Two bullets hit two walls at opposite ends of the tunnel.

"Please try, Victoria." I grabbed her head and looked right into her eyes, let my busted nose touch her own. She leaned in closer, trembling. Her tears were warm and wet against my cheek. "Please. For Gabe."

Finally, she nodded. "Okay. For Gabe. Give me . . . the other gun."

That kinda stunned me, but hell if I wasn't happy to hear she was willing to fight. "Do you know how to fire it?"

"No. But I'll figure it out."

I handed her Mr. Budweiser's pistol and made sure the safety was off. "Here. There are fifteen shots in the clip. If you fire, fire controlled. Don't unload the whole thing on nothing."

She knuckled the tears from her face and started sliding toward the door.

I watched her open it, slide through, and then leaned out to check for Bob again. He was nowhere in sight, which could mean he was pressed back in the alcove—could be another tunnel for all I knew—or had scrambled up the ladder.

"Come on, stick your head out," I said.

Several seconds passed but he didn't lean out.

Time to go, I thought, and fired off a warning shot just to keep him at bay.

The door had swung shut behind Victoria, so I threw it open and ran down the tunnel after her. I didn't see her, which meant she'd already made it to the basement.

"Fast girl."

When I reached the other end I heard Bob behind me in the cage room, swearing. As much as I wanted to wait for him to come into the tunnel so I could shoot him down, I wasn't so sure my aim right now was steady enough to hit him. Instead, I emerged into the dark basement—which wasn't so dark anymore. An overhead light had been turned on at the other end, back near the stairs up to the kitchen. Suddenly I was surrounded by the most crazy-eyed dancing wolves you've ever seen.

I let out a stifled cry and reflexively aimed at the nearest one, hoping to shoot it in the head. Thank God I didn't because I realized it was just a statue. There were tons of them, large and small, waving swords, holding up bones.

"Victoria?" I whispered, maneuvering through the statues looking for her. "Where are you? It's me, Roger." How I hadn't run into these things the first time through in the dark is a miracle. Why did they all only have one eye?

Movement. To my right. I spun, gun raised, saw a man in a black suit step behind one of the statues. He was mostly bald with a thin

ring of white hair over his ears. Had he nodded at me before he
skirted out of view?

I was pretty sure he did, and it pretty much came across as an
acknowledgment of some game of cat and mouse. Great, now I
had two of these freaks on my tail.

I drifted left, away from the stairs, hoping to cut a wide circle
around and back.

Another movement. The bald man in the suit stepped out into
view up ahead. He whispered something inaudible. Looked like . .
. well, it looked like he said my name. *Roger.* How did he know me?

I hadn't seen him in the dining room earlier. He was not one of
Marshall's cannibal friends, unless he was a late arrival. I supposed
he could have been staff, maybe a butler or something, but he
seemed out of place somehow.

"Roger?" Victoria's voice broke me from my trance. It was
coming from somewhere near the stairs.

"Victoria? Stay put. Hide."

"Roger!" Her scream bounced off the walls. It was a scream of
pain and fear, no longer concerned with stealth or hiding. It was
followed by obvious signs of a struggle. Grunts, huffing, legs kicking, what sounded like a slap. Shit, they'd found her.

I rounded two more statues, gun at the ready, prepared to plug
holes in whomever was wrestling her, saw her bare legs just a few
yards ahead of me jutting out from behind more bad art. I also saw
the man in the suit to my right. He was just watching, composed like
a spectator at the theater. Then there were stars as Bob charged out
from behind the nearest wolf, tackled me to the ground, and
slammed his elbow into my chest. The gun slid from my hands, my
muscles took a vacation. My own Red Sox cap fell off his fat head
and onto my face, and I could smell the sweat he'd already left inside it. A hot gun muzzle pressed against my temple, burned the
skin above my ear with an audible crackle. I was in too much of a
daze to scream.

The hammer cocked back.

"No! Alive, keep him alive."

Through the murky haze of near death and partially obstructed
vision through the baseball hat, I saw Ben holding Victoria. "I need
to question him."

"Let me kill this fucker," Bob said. He took the hat off my face and put it back on his own head.

"You're not even supposed to still be here." Ben had Victoria in a strangle hold; he was holding the gun I'd given her. Her feet kicked wildly as her breath cut out.

"I was waiting for Cary."

"Your friend left a while ago."

"No, he didn't. He said he was getting something from the van and coming back. Only he never came back. He don't run off on me. We were taking the van back together, gonna get a beer. I climbed up the ladder a minute ago and saw him up there dead with a gardening tool in his neck. And I know this shit did it, so I want to kill his ass."

"Well, there's a change of plans. I need to know if anyone else knows this guy is here. Marshall has rules about this kind of thing."

Bob frisked me as impatiently as he could muster. "He ain't got a phone."

"Fine, we'll put them back in the cages. Marshall will be down for her in a few minutes. We'll need to sedate her again. He doesn't like them to scream when the ritual begins."

"What? Keep him alive?"

"I'm not going to tell you again, Bob. Pick him up and lock him in the cages."

"Fine." Bob socked me in the eye and I thought my head would go through the floor. My damn nose was already so swollen I didn't think I'd ever be able to smell again, and his punch once more shifted the broken bones around. As I've already said, some pains are just so intense you can't scream for fear of making them hurt more. That punch was one of those kinds.

He lifted me off the floor and dragged me back through the ugly statues toward the homemade dungeon. I heard Victoria behind me, sobbing in her captor's arms.

So close, Roger. So damned close, but no cigar.

They threw us in separate cages and locked the door to the hallway. Now we were all in the dungeon. While Ben checked the locks on the cages Bob sat in the chair again, in the middle of the room, leering at me. He was pissed beyond belief.

I leaned back against the rear of the cage, felt the hard dirt wall

behind it, briefly wondering if I could tunnel my way to the outside
world should I be able to bend the bars wide enough apart. Maybe
with enough time and a tire jack, but Bob wasn't going to let me out
of his sight.

"Take a picture, Bob," I said.

"You do realize Marshall is gonna kill you."

"I dunno, he looked pretty stuffed last time I saw him."

Bob's reaction to that was a little funny. I think he thought I
was making some joke that he wasn't getting. It begged the question
of whether or not Bob knew what was going on upstairs.

"You partake of these dinners too, Bob?" I asked.

"I already ate."

"Don't you know you can get all types of diseases eating human
flesh?"

Again, he cocked his head kind of funny.

"Enough!" Ben said. He withdrew a pair of small wire cutters
from his pocket. "You talk again and I will remove a finger."

Ben stepped back next to Bob. "And that goes for you too, Bob.
Once we're done here you leave this house and stay gone."

"Yeah, well, guess I get all the money this time," he said with a
smile, "so I ain't got a problem with that. Mark my word, boy, if Ben
and Marshall don't kill you, I will find you and make you suffer."

I looked at Ben. "He's still talking. Take his thumb." For a moment Ben stopped and looked at me like he was going to come in
and really do some damage to me, but then Victoria whimpered
and he remembered he had other work to do. Over near the door
was a first aid kit. I hadn't seen it before because sometimes it's hard
to notice things when you're being shot at. He opened it up and
took out a syringe and a little bottle of something nefarious. He
filled the syringe with the liquid and entered the other cage with
Victoria.

"No," she pleaded, and tried to back up out of the way. Ben
caught her by the shirt, lifting it up so I could see her scarred thighs
and bruised womanhood, and jammed the needle into her shoulder.
She didn't squirm much, just sort of took it out of fear. To be safe,
Ben put a hand over her mouth and flattened himself against her
to keep her from moving. It only took a few seconds for her to fall
forward in his arms, her eyes rolling back in her head.

"Ain't that a sight," Bob said, licking his lips.

"What did you give her?" I asked. As if I'm some kind of doctor and would know whatever drug was in the needle anyway.

Bob pointed at me. "He talked, Ben. Take off a finger."

"You talked first," I replied. "Fair is fair, Ben, take his first."

"I did not talk first!"

"Did too. You said it was a pretty sight."

"Listen, you little—Ow!"

Ben smacked Bob in the back of the head. "Shut it! Both of you." Then to Bob specifically: "Just sit here while I talk. Can you do that?"

Bob nodded, rubbing the back of his head.

Ben unlocked the cage door with the ring of keys on his belt, came in and stood over me. "Give me your hand."

"No."

He pointed the gun at me and I figured it would be a swifter death than the wire cutters would grant me so I didn't really flinch. "I can shoot you in your dick and then take your hand. Understand?"

Yeah, well, he had a point there. Not that my dick saw much action in my life but I kind of liked it where it was. I held my hand out to him in a fist.

He grabbed it and twisted it sideways near to its breaking point. Now I flinched because it frigging hurt.

"How did you get in?" he asked.

"Back door. It was unlocked."

"Must have been Cary," Bob said, then went tightlipped.

"Who knows you're here?"

"Everybody. The cops, the president, your mother—Ah!"

I heard something pop in my wrist as he twisted harder. "Tell me what you've seen?"

"Saw the buffet upstairs, if that's what you mean. Saw Marshall and his friends eat that girl alive."

At this Bob went a bit wide-eyed. I guess he hadn't known what was going on upstairs after all.

"Did you, now? And do you know who you are dealing with?"

"Look, I just needed to take a piss, saw the door open and came in to use the bathroom. I have a really bad memory so you can just let me go and forget this whole thing. Cool?"

"You're brave, boy, but not as brave as you think."

"'Boy?' I'm thirty. Don't you see the gray hairs on my head?"

"If anyone is coming after you, or if anyone else is here with you, you're death will take days. Tell the truth now and I can make it swift."

"The truth is I'm used to this type of situation . . . so do your worst."

"Fine. I will assume you have complicated things for us tonight, which is going to make Marshall very unhappy. The police were already here once and I suspect you have something to do with it. I will be back in a bit, and when I come, we will see how long you can hold out. I will even let Bob join in."

With that he went back and carried Victoria out of her cage. He took my shirt off her and threw it on the ground, then carried her unconscious body back out toward the cellar, leaving me alone with Bob.

"Just you and me, buddy," Bob said when the hallway door closed. "Just you and me and this here gun and, oh, look, some drugs to make you a little sleepy."

Chapter 17

Time seemed to speed up now, the seconds bursting away in my mind like a lit brick of firecrackers. Bangbangbangbang. Gone. I was trapped in a cage in a room with a guy who wanted to beat me alive, the girl I was in love with was on her way upstairs to be eaten, and there was a house full of maniacs surrounding me. All I could do was curse God, pray that Victoria would be saved by a miracle. Helplessness is the worst feeling in the world, especially when you know your own inabilities mean someone else's pain. It all felt so unfair.

But what could I do? There were no police procedurals that I knew of for getting out of this type of situation. You basically needed Michael Bay to write some really convenient plot twist, and Will Smith to be muscular enough to carry it out, so that the film ends on a high.

Now welcome back to real life.

I reached up and tenderly felt my nose to gauge how bad it was. The word grapefruit came to mind. A glance at my wrist showed it was swollen as well. Maybe not broken, but sprained at least. Felt like the tendons had crisscrossed under the skin. It was my right hand, the one I aimed with, so that was not a good thing. I flexed my finger to make sure they could still move, and they did, but it sent fire all the way up to my shoulder.

Good ol' Bob was being his usual idiot self and went and got the first aid kit, took out the needle and filled it with whatever knockout juice was in the little bottle.

"Only a little," he said. "Wouldn't want you to miss the experience."

"Tooth," I said quietly, "if you're listening, if you've been hanging around and I'm really not crazy, I could use some help. I know I've asked you a bunch tonight and maybe that was you with the mosquito and the road sign, maybe not, but either way, help me out. I mean, he's got your hat, man."

"The fuck you talking to?"

"Imaginary friend. You're wearing his old hat. Just thought he might like it back. So how are we gonna do this? You coming in here or should I go out there?"

He took his gun out of his waistband. "Funny. You stay right there behind them bars. Stick your foot out so I can inject you."

"Are you serious? You think I'm going to do what you want? You're not that stupid. How well did you do in school?"

"Fuck school. Dropped out."

"You're kidding me. Took you for a scholar. You remind me of a teacher I—"

Bang!

The bullet threw me backwards and slammed me into the wall, knocking the breath out of me. I'm pretty sure I screamed but I was so far beyond broken-nose pain at this point I couldn't even be sure it was me. I slumped down to my ass, waiting to die, thinking of Victoria upstairs, but could still feel myself breathing. I looked at my chest and realized I hadn't been hit there, but rather in the left arm. It was a big red mess and it hurt like hell.

"You'll live," Bob said, laughing, "just a flesh wound. It's only a 9mm. Hurts like a bitch though, huh?"

It was more than a flesh wound, believe me, it was a crater in my left bicep. Blood was pumping out so fast I felt it running down my sides into my pants.

"Well, maybe it's more than a flesh wound. I don't have the best aim. Now stick your foot out."

I suddenly felt sick to my stomach. You might think you're tough but in this type of situation you eventually cave. Bullets hurt like nothing you can imagine, and they can kill you. And no matter how many times I wish for death to just take me out of this crappy, violence-filled life, I still have an innate sense of self-preservation. If letting Bob inject me with a sedative was going to prolong my life, I was going to take it. I've said this before, but wishing for death and actually letting yourself die are two totally different animals. I wish it wasn't so.

Wincing, I slid my foot out of the bars as I pressed my sprained hand against the bullet wound in my arm, trying to staunch the blood and just generally hoping that holding my hand there would ease the pain.

Bob bent down near my foot and flicked the tip of the needle with his finger to get the air out. Why the hell he cared about that precaution was beyond me. The idiot probably just saw doctors do it on hospital TV dramas and figured it was part of giving someone a shot. What did he care if he gave me an embolism?

"Hold up," I said, my heart just about ripping through my chest now. It was all I could do to generate saliva in my mouth.

"What? I ain't gonna kill you yet, just have a little fun."

"What about Ben?"

"He just wants to talk to you some more. I'll leave enough of you for that. He won't care. And if he does, so what? I have my fail-safes in place in case something goes wrong with these people tonight. See, I'm not as big of a moron as you think."

"I dunno, I'm thinking pretty big. But what about that guy at the door?" There was a face peeking in at us. It was the same guy I had seen in the basement, the bald guy with the black suit.

Bob turned his head to look, saw the guy, said, "Who the . . . ?"

That was when I kicked. My foot hit Bob's hand and drove the syringe up and into the bottom of his chin. He screamed and yanked it out immediately, but it was too late. I saw the plunger had pushed up. Was it enough? I hoped so.

The face at the door suddenly disappeared and I was betting dollars to donuts whoever it was was on their way upstairs to report what just happened. My life was just one happy ticking clock after another.

"Son of a . . . bitch," Bob moaned, his voice slurring. "Why did . . . you . . . do that?"

He blinked a few times, then raised the gun at me, staggering a bit.

"Wait! What about Ben!"

He didn't' care. He squeezed the trigger. I threw my hands up in front of my face. But the drug was fast and he sort of fell sideways as he fired, hit the cage next to mine and dropped to the ground. The bullet pinged off one of the bars and ricocheted into the wall near the first aid kit.

I moved as quickly as I could, reaching through the bars with

my good arm, and grabbed the gun out of his hand. He was fighting the effects of the drug and tried to hold on to it but his muscles weren't really obeying him. I yanked it away. One shot at the
cage's lock set me free, but the recoil of the gun jerked my ruined
wrist backwards enough that I dropped the gun and screamed in
pain. Firing it again was going to be tough; I had one useless arm
on my left side and a bum hand on the right. I picked it back up anyway because I sure as shit wasn't going to leave it around for Bob
to get and, well, you know, I wasn't going to get very far without it.

On the floor in front of me Bob was trying to get to his knees
with eyes half closed and a mouth that was a big drooling maw. I
stepped over him, took my hat off his head and put the gun to his
head. He rolled over and looked at me with a sort of resignation
that almost made me mad. "What're you . . . some fucking . . . superhero?" I fixed the Red Sox cap on my head once more. "If I
was a superhero I'd bring you to the police, Bob. But you don't deserve such niceties. But tell you what, I won't kill you. You're too pathetic and defenseless lying here like this. I'm not cold-blooded."

"You'd better . . . kill . . . me or . . ."

"Stop talking, Bob. I'm not gonna kill you, but I won't live
knowing what you did to Victoria, knowing what you like to do to
girls."

I lowered the gun, looked into his eyes, and shot him in the
dick.

Twice.

Warm blood spit up and stained my face. There was something
satisfying in that. Almost made me forget the agonizing pain I felt
in my wrist once more.

Oh, man how he wailed. Even in his drugged-up state, he was
like a deafening siren, holding his hands to his crotch and rolling
back and forth like a man on fire. Before I left the room I took a
look at his downstairs area and saw nothing but gristle. The mound
of bloody meat that had been his genitalia was now on the floor,
blown into bits near his knees. He rolled over onto it as he screamed
and squished it all.

"Fuck you, Bob. See you around."

I grabbed my shirt and left.

The door to the underground hallway was easily opened from

inside. I was back in the basement in a heartbeat, weaving through those weird statues again. Wolf upon wolf upon wolf, this one with a spear, this one with a sword, that one with an ax. I tied the shirt around my arm wound as I went. It helped stop the blood flow, but just barely.

The layout of the basement was becoming familiar to me now, at least this part of it. Where the other rooms and hallways went I didn't care. I found the stairs leading back up to the kitchen and took them slowly, listening for movement or breathing from above. Nothing told me anyone was waiting for me but that didn't mean a surprise wasn't ready to pounce on me from the top.

Ben was obviously a fool to trust Bob because he hadn't locked the door at the top. For that matter, neither had the strange man in black who'd spied on me in the cages. Or maybe it just didn't have a lock. Who knows?

I pushed it open into the kitchen once again, hearing the familiar chamber music coming out over the house's PA system. As quickly and quietly as I could I maneuvered back down the servant hallway toward the room with my painting. Soon I was back near the chaise lounge I'd hidden behind earlier, looking into the dining room, which was now empty. They'd said something about going up to the Observatory, and since I had no better leads I figured I'd find Victoria there. I stopped once, skulking past the dining room, to pick up a phone that sat on an antique cabinet near a room with an impressive Steinway piano. Call me brave but I'm not stupid. I needed to get the police back here stat.

There was no dial tone.

"Surprise, Roger. That would be too easy," I said.

I went further down, listening for goons with guns. A wide staircase was directly in front of me down the hall, the kind of staircase rich people love to walk down in expensive clothes. A plush red runner ran up the center of the stairs as if it ascended toward some type of throne room.

I checked behind me to make sure no one was coming, saw the trail of blood I'd left from the gunshot in my arm. "Great."

I went up, step by step, sticking to the side, letting my arm bleed through the shirt bandage all over the expensive woodwork. Voices suddenly became audible as I went higher. There was laughing, burping, general merriment. The cocktail party of the damned was still in full swing, and dessert was on the way. When I was nearly at the second floor I stopped in the middle of the staircase, my eyes were level with the floor ahead of me, and I saw one of the gun-toting goons pacing in the wide hallway. If I'd had a silencer I might have shot him but then again the vibrations of his massive body hitting the floor would have shaken the house like an earthquake and driven everyone in a panic right to me.

There was something about this goon's eyes that frightened me, something focused. Unlike when I'd seen him earlier, this guy looked a bit twitchy, as if he were on guard. Which of course made sense if Ben had told his underlings someone had been captured sneaking around the house. He had that shoot-first-ask-questions-later look in his eyes.

You sure you don't want to just shoot him in the face, Murderboy? You've racked up quite the body count tonight as it is. Your bloodlust rivals even my own. Soon enough you'll be raping and cutting, and I'll be right by your side, waiting to congratulate you.

"Not real," I whispered. Pressing my fingers to my nose shut off Skinny Man's voice for a second but he was back lickity split.

Imagine if your lovely sis was still alive. The things we could do to her to-gether. The things we could stick in her. Like the razor wire I used to cut through her cunt to her ass. You know, the razor wire I wrapped your buddy's head with.

Need my meds, I thought. *Holy crap I need to get back on the meds, I don't care what Dr. Marsh said.*

The guard in front of me was suddenly met by another goon, and together they talked for a few seconds. I couldn't hear what they were saying, but there were some hand movements that looked like directives. Somehow I was keeping time in my head—ten seconds, twenty seconds, thirty seconds—and started willing them to move off to another hallway less I fail to make it to the third floor before Victoria was laid on a table.

I don't know if it was my Force powers or what, but they did break up and move down to another corridor. They had their guns raised as if they'd heard something or were stalking someone. Didn't matter to me what they were after or what their motives were for moving, it gave me a window of opportunity to rush up to the next flight of stairs. As I rounded the railing I caught sight of something startling in a mirror on the wall.

I saw Tooth.

Well, what looked like Tooth, wearing his Red Sox cap. I'm sure it was just me. I mean, I was wearing the cap now, and I am prone to strange voices and hallucinations when I'm not on my meds. I've been talking to him and seeing him for ten years now. Yeah, I'm loco.

Still, it looked an awful lot like Tooth.

On the middle landing of this set of stairs was another one of those creepy wolf statues. This one was a bit more hybridized than the others I'd seen, with different animal parts for arms and legs, maybe part horse or deer, I couldn't tell. It had one massive eye above a wide, fanged mouth, and someone had draped a red sash over its shoulders. It was holding a woman's head and howling up to the ceiling. This one was also anatomically correct—which they all may have been for all I'd noticed—with a massive barbed dick that hung down to its knees.

There were words carved into the stone base, but I couldn't read the language. Lots of Ks and Cs and Vs which made me think it was Slavic or something. That word was in there again: PSOGLAV. The one from the painting downstairs.

Marshall's voice drifted down to me, quiet and rushed, and I realized he was in the room right off the hallway at the top of the stairs.

"I don't want anyone here to know what's going on in the basement. I've gone to great pains to have this night be a release for all of us and I will not have some fucking kid ruining it."

"Yes, Marshall." Ben's voice. They were obviously discussing me.

"Keep the little shit locked up in the cage until after the guests leave. Then I want to talk to him. You didn't drug him, did you?"

"No, sir."

"Good. Keep him lucid so he can speak freely and feel whatever pain I need to bring to his world to get my answers. If he's compromised my position in this community I will destroy every relative he has before I finish him myself."

"I don't trust him down there alone with that criminal buffoon."

"What criminal buffoon? One of Barry's men?"

"Yeah. Bob. He's watching the kid down there but I got a feeling he's gonna do something stupid. I don't think he should even be here. What if he sees something?"

"Well of course he shouldn't still be here! Why haven't you told him to leave?"

"He said he was waiting for one of the other guys. Found him dead out back."

"Dead? You've checked this out?"

"I sent someone to check on it a minute ago. Haven't heard back yet."

"Well, this Bob is no doubt to blame for this sudden turn in events. Wait until we've had dessert—I want you here in case there is an issue—then go down and kill the idiot. Kill him in front of my uninvited guest so he knows how serious his situation is. Barry will have to hire new help from now on but that's not really my concern. Now, where *is* the dessert?"

"I have her in the next room. She's out cold."

"I trust you gave her the requisite dosage."

"Same as always, sir."

"Fine. Bring her in already so I can get on with my party."

"Yes, sir."

I heard them leave, moving off in different directions. Marshall was now explaining something about the lens on his telescope to someone, and whoever it was seemed mighty interested.

I crept up to the top of the stairs, saw the party through the doorway to my right. It was a large room with floor-to-ceiling windows, a full bar, some antique globes and one heck of a nice telescope in the center. Through the windows I saw the bright blue moon above the surrounding foothills. The lighting in the room was low, probably to diminish the room's reflection in the windows so one could see the stars outside, but I was still able to get an idea of where people were. This room stretched down to the other end of the house, and most of the guests were at that other end.

I squatted low outside the entrance and peeked my head around the jamb, saw the white-haired bitch, Belle, sipping wine, saw the fat man looking through the telescope, saw the others in a conversational circle near some leather recliners, and counted four nameless goons with guns surrounding another well-dressed table. Ten bucks said there was cold metal with basins underneath the table-cloth.

Funny thing about the scene was that, again, it looked normal if you discounted the blood-stained faces and dresses and suits coated in bits of female flesh. The sick bastards hadn't even bothered to clean themselves. But then why bother? They were about to eat again and would just make another mess.

The bar was on my side, sharing the common wall with the long hallway my ass was in. Marshall's wife was playing bartender, opening another bottle of wine now. She poured some full glasses and stuck them at the end of the bar.

Shit! I ducked back out. One of the goons had just looked my way. I couldn't tell if he saw me or not but I couldn't stay around to find out.

I bolted to a room off the hallway, away from the stairs, some kind of storage room with plenty of boxes in it. Flicking the light on would give me away so I couldn't tell what was in the boxes, but I can tell you they smelled bad. Smelled a lot like sweat and mold.

When I risked a glance back toward the stairs sure enough that goon had come over and stuck his head out, looking at the stairs, which was enough time for me to stick my own head back in. I'd left quite a blood trail on the floor, but the lighting was low and the hall rug was brown, so I hoped and prayed it would disappear. If he noticed it, would it register as a new stain? I had to think these guys saw a lot of blood around this house. I waited to see if he'd come down my way, all the while holding my arm and dripping sweat. My insides were hurting and my head was getting dizzy. Blood loss will do that to you. My entire left half was going a bit numb and while that helped me stand the pain of the bullet in my arm, it concerned me greatly. If I passed out both Victoria and I were dead meat.

The goon didn't come my way. After a few seconds I peeked back out again and saw the doorway was empty. He either went down the stairs or back into the room.

There was a cheer from the observatory across the hall, and I heard Marshall say, "Ah, dessert has arrived."

Chapter 18

No no no no no, I thought. Not good. This was not good at all. Four guys with guns that would make Rambo jealous, five guys if Ben was back in there, and a roomful of cannibals. Worse, right wing cannibals with money and influence.

I slid the clip out of the gun, checked the bullet counter. Six shots left. My mind raced with possibilities: run in and shoot all five goons in the head, and then Marshall? Yeah right, my right hand still throbbed from when Ben had twisted it and I was woozy from a bullet wound. Not to mention my broken nose had me seeing halos around everything. I probably couldn't hit the broad side of a barn from ten feet away. Run in, hold Marshall hostage and hope the gunmen couldn't shoot me over his shoulder? Marshall would just tell them to shoot. He seemed like that kind of egomaniac. Run in and just take out as many as I could before I got plugged? Well, that wasn't going to save Victoria no matter how many I shot.

As usual, I found myself turning to the things I knew best: comics and movies and video games. Most notably the last one, because the one thing in life I was good at, besides painting fucking trees, giving my money to therapists, and talking to dead people, was kicking ass at First-person Shooters. Back in the day, Tooth and I would go toe-to-toe on *Counter Strike* and *Medal of Honor* and I would whoop his butt.

"You're fucking cheating, dickstain," he would yell. "You've modded your keyboard."

"You just don't think ahead. You gotta anticipate the opponents' moves. I know what gamers are gonna do before they do it."

"Well have a cookie and celebrate yourself. I'm thinking of pussy and you're thinking of where some ten-year-old with a joystick is hiding in Nazi Germany. I bet you even think about whether or not his balls have dropped yet? Got that one all figured out, Darth 'Bator?"

Tooth was always a sore loser.

So what's the first thing you do in a game when you need to take out a room full of enemies? You get a big gun. And where do you find a big gun? You take it from the enemy that's holding it.

That was about the best plan I was going to come up with, and if I didn't execute it fast I was probably going to lie down right here and sleep forever next to the boxes.

I slinked out of the room, this time heading toward the far end of the hall, away from the stairs, hoping to take the goon just inside the rear door to the Observation Room by surprise. I'd shoot him in the leg, grab his gun, and do my best to get the others before they knew what was happening. Like a video game I planned it out as I walked. Take out the first guy; shoot the second; duck behind the bar and scurry to the other end of it; stay low; lean out and get the third and fourth guy; then back out into the hallway where I'd wait for number five.

It would have worked great in a video game, but I wasn't so lucky. I slipped in, saw the first goon right in front of me, and then felt an elephant's trunk around my neck. I went flaccid and felt the gun yanked from my hand.

Ben had come out of nowhere. "You are a brave little man."

The guests all turned and gasped.

"Marshall, is there a problem?" asked the judge. "Who is this young man?"

Marshall waved it all off in his customary fashion. "Nothing, nothing, just a minor inconvenience. We're taking care of it. Ben, please remove our new guest to his quarters. And try not to get his blood everywhere. That arm looks dreadful."

"Is it an intruder?" The judge again.

"Unfortunately, Judge, but he's alone, not to worry."

"How can you be sure?"

"He's not," I said around chokes. "I called everyone I know and told them—"

Ben cut off my words with a tightening of his baboon arm.

"Marshall, I dare say this is not the ideal moment for unwanted guests."

"I am taking care of it, Your Honor."

At this point I saw Victoria on the table. They'd taken the table cloth off just like in the dining room downstairs. She was shackled to it, unconscious, her eyes still closed. Her naked body was bruised and I could see the streaks around her eyes from a lifetime of crying. Two men were already sitting at the table, knives and forks in hand. One of them, more interested in his meal than in me, was poking her breast with his fork.

Flashbacks of Skinny Man's basement materialized out of nowhere, and suddenly I was crying. All my bravado had jumped ship and left me to beg like it was ten years ago in some madman's basement. "Please don't kill her. Please don't. She didn't do anything."

"Of course she hasn't done anything," Marshall said. "She doesn't need to have done anything. She just needs to have what we want. Her youth, her spirit, her light."

"You're all fucking sick! You're going to go to Hell for this!"

"My boy, we aren't going to Hell or anywhere else. That's the whole point here, don't you see? This is an offering to our lord, who keeps us in good health."

"You're all fucking nuts."

"And you, boy, have betrayed yourself. You know this girl here, as is evident, but for you to be here alone means you knew where she was and couldn't get anyone to help you. Am I right? Otherwise you wouldn't be so dumb as to stick around. See, Judge, this is why we don't dine on his kind."

"Dreadful bitter is the man meat," said the white haired woman.

"Just don't eat her," I said. "Not alive. Not like that." My head was spinning, Ben was cutting off my air, my arm was dripping blood albeit less torrentially than before, and my face was so swollen I could see my own forehead in my upper peripheral.

"Oh, we're going to eat her . . . what is your name?"

Ben jerked me around and dug a knuckle into my ribs. It hurt like hell and did the trick. "Roger."

"Roger what?"

"Smith."

"Does he have a wallet, Ben?"

Ben frisked me. "No."

I'd forgotten all about my wallet, couldn't even remember which kidnapper had taken it. Getting back my Red Sox hat was of more concern to me than my credit cards. At least I'd gotten it back.

"No matter," said Marshall. "We'll get it out of you later. I can see by your swollen face you've had about as much pain as you're going to be able to take. You'll talk rather quickly when we work on your nose and . . . is that a bullet wound? I can certainly use that. Ben, take him back down and—"

"No," said the judge, stepping toward me. The room seemed to get even quieter as he moved, as if the other guests were awed by his stride. "Let him watch. He went through all this trouble to find his friend here, I think the least we can do is let him have closure."

Marshall looked to his wife for a second, who nodded approval, then smiled. "Excellent idea. Roger, do please join us for dinner."

Ben shoved me forward toward the table and forced me into one of the seats. The other four goons, who had circled us as soon as Ben got his arm around me, trained their weapons at my head.

The white-haired bird sat on my right, the judge on my left, the fat man directly across from me. Everyone else took their seats as well, with Marshall and his wife at the heads of the table.

"Don't do this, Marshall," I said. "I told everyone what's going on here. I saw Barry before I came. He's dead by the way. I'm the one who sent the police earlier and I called Sheriff Ted Mathers in New Hampshire and told him if I don't check in that he should send the cavalry here. Go ahead, look it all up, see if I'm lying."

For a moment I thought I could see a sliver of fear in Marshall's eyes. Most good businessmen can tell when a person is lying or telling the truth, and everything I'd just told him was one hundred percent accurate. But good businessmen, much like chess champions, are able to weigh the outcome of a move and see how it will play out ten moves in the future.

"The police are already convinced you were a prank call," he said. "I will have to wait to find out about Barry. If he is dead, I certainly won't lose sleep. As for a sheriff in New Hampshire . . . by the time he's secured any agreements by local authorities to ask me more questions everything you see here will be long discarded. I fund most of the police force in this town, and my friend here Judge Coates is a friend as well. May I ask what it is you do for a living, boy? Exactly how do you know Barry?"

"Didn't say I knew him, just said he was dead."

"You said you saw Barry, which I take to mean you called on him. So you do know him. How? Through the gallery? It would explain how you know of this beautiful girl before us."

I was seated at Victoria's right hip, trying not to stare at the soft skin of her belly and thighs, and especially her wounded womanhood.

"Answer the man," the judge said. He was rubbing his fork and knife together right next to me. *Scritch scritch scritch.* "Unless you want to be found in contempt."

Judge Coates smiled at his own lame joke.

"I paint. You've bought my stuff. In fact, I want it back."

The white-haired bird chuckled and leaned her bulbous face into mine. "So you are an artist? That's wonderful. What type of stuff do you paint?" As she spoke I looked at her bloodstained teeth and thought about punching them down her throat.

"I paint old cunts like you getting shot in the face."

She was unfazed by my attempt to shock her. I guess if you're going to eat people alive you can pretty much deal with curses and gory imagery.

"I should like to see such a painting, in fact," she said. "There is so much power and strength that comes from the taking of another's soul, but I assume you're just trying to make me flinch. Isn't he a scream, Marshall? Maybe after we dine on your girlfriend here Marshall will let me take you to my house and I can show you a good time."

There was an image that actually scared *me*. "You're sick. Ugly, old and sick."

Now she leaned in even closer and whispered in my ear. "If I had my way I'd take you home and fuck your ass with my sewing shears." She leaned back, giggling.

If Skinny Man were still alive I could have hooked him up on a date with this old nutbag.

"Who shot you?" Marshall asked. "You look about on your last leg."

"He wasn't shot when I left him," Ben said. "Must have been that idiot down in the basement."

"Yeah, he's dead too," I said.

Marshall checked his watch for a second. "No matter, saves Ben the job of having to do it himself. If you would be so kind as to put your arm over the table so the blood doesn't get on the floor."

I looked at him. "Are you serious?"

One of the goons grabbed my left arm and slammed it on the table. White hot pain lashed up my neck and made my brain swell. I tried hard not to scream but my shaking gave away my hurt, which made everyone around me smile like they were watching a comedy film.

The fat man across from me poked Victoria in the ribs, licked his finger. "How much longer until she wakes?"

"Any second now," Marshall replied. "Does anyone need more wine?"

"Don't do this," I pleaded again. "Please, don't do this. This is wrong, this is sick, this is . . ."

"My boy, this is the way of the world."

"What world! You eat people! This isn't the way of the world, this is a party for asylum inmates! Please don't do this!"

"Shh. No need to yell. We're right here. We need her to honor our lord, to give us new life, so that we may continue to keep the community in the black. We couldn't let rabble like you swoop in and take it over, with your rock music and gangs and drugs. We've made this town the affluent circle it is, and we have no desire to stop."

"Fuck your community. You're all psychos, sick psychos who'll burn in Hell."

"Oh, Hell is not a fear for us, Roger. Hell is a place of power that will welcome us with open arms. You really have wandered into the wrong house tonight. You've ruined my party and upset my guests and for that there will be punishment. But before we have our talk later you will see just how beneficial Hell can be."

Victoria stirred.

Everyone at the table stared down at her with eager grins, picked up their utensils and licked their lips.

"Give it a second," Marshall sad. "Wait until her eyes open."

"No!" I leapt up and tried to shove my way to Marshall but the goons grabbed me and slammed me down.

"Hold him!" Marshall yelled. "He moves again shoot him in the legs." Then looking back at Victoria, his own hands raised with fork and knife: "Any second now."

Her legs twitched, her shoulder moved, she made a little noise the way people do when they wake up, and then her eyes opened. The drug was still overwhelming her, and she was so out of it she wasn't even confused, just trying to wake up fully. She looked down at me, and I think she recognized me in some back room of her mind.

"Bon appétit," said Marshall.

At once the dinner guests groaned and jammed their knives into Victoria's soft flesh. Blades slipped into her belly, her thighs, her breasts, and one through her cheek. Blood arced out and she immediately shivered like someone forcing themselves out of a nightmare.

Oh, how I screamed, how I shook, how I flailed. Four strong arms held me down while guns pressed hard into my back.

The knives started cutting, opening long gouges in her flawless skin. The blood was running onto the table now as they sawed into her. Victoria was looking right at me, the glaze in her eyes dissipating as reality—confusing as it must be—began to set in.

"Such a beautiful catch," Belle said.

I did the only thing I could think to do. With my one good arm I put my hand under the lip of the table and shoved.

Let's get this straight right now: I am not a superhero. I love superheroes, love comics, love movies, but I know the difference between the real world and make-believe. *Lena 12* was my first foray into comics and I'd chosen to make her a space assassin rather than a superhero with alien powers because Skinny Man had proven to me that heroes never come to rescue you. Batman or Spider-Man or Superman do not swoop in and save the day when you're faced with death, or worse, torture. You're at the mercy of your wits or your captor's ineptitude. If you're lucky, you've been taught survival skills and have the wherewithal to apply them in stressful moments.

But here's the thing. When I grabbed the edge of the table I felt stronger than I ever had in my whole life. Inhumanly strong, like superhero strong. You read stories sometimes about people who

show incredible feats of strength when put in deadly situations—
they lift cars, break down doors, jump really high. Call it an abnor-
mal burst of adrenaline but it works. It's like having a superpower.

I grabbed the edge of the table and flipped it over with one
arm. It came crashing down onto the sickos sitting across from me,
Victoria still strapped underneath, now pinned between the table
top and the bodies of the dinner party trying to eat her. At once
everyone jumped back from their seats and yelled, creating a small
mob that brought confusion and zigzag activity. I didn't have time
to hear what they were saying, because I was slamming my already-
mashed up head back into the goon behind me, kicking myself up
and backwards with all my might and taking us both down to the
ground.

I felt something slam into my side and heard one of my own
ribs crack, almost passing out from the agonizing pain. Someone
was hitting me with something metal, maybe one of the guns or a
lead pipe. Who knows? It hurt but I was in a blind rage and pushed
it aside.

Underneath me the goon grabbed my neck and tried to knock
me out but I reached out and found his gun, his finger still on the
trigger, and squeezed. Bullets cracked and people screamed, suddenly running away from the fight.

I was lifted off of the goon by two others, but as I felt myself
hoisted into the air, the gunman on the floor shot at me, completely
missing, and hit the goon on my right in the face which tore open
a hole under his eyes large enough for me to put my fist in. All three
of us fell sideways, Marshall screaming to "stop shooting!" and I
landed right on the faceless man's gun, squeezed the trigger and hit
the goon on the floor in the chest.

The white-haired woman, in her effort to get out of the line of
fire, tripped and fell on top of us, her scaly arm fat covering my face.

"Stop shooting! Everybody stop firing!" Marshall's voice somewhere in the room.

I heard the stampede around me, saw shiny black shoes and high
heels running by my face, heard the table being moved, heard chairs
squeaking and falling, Ben shouting something, a gun cocking.

I fired again, making the third goon jump off of me, and leapt
to my feet. Ben aimed at me through panicked dinner guests, and I

ran to the bar, automatic weapon dangling upside down in my hand.

Ben's bullets skimmed my hair and hit the giant mirror behind the bar as I leapt over the bar top and landed on the floor behind it, thankfully on my right arm, though the pain was still damn near unbearable.

"Stop fucking firing! Everybody calm down! Ben, just kill him and be done with it," Marshall said. He had changed his mind about having a talk with me. That can happen when you're dealing with party crashers like myself, I guess. It was fine with me. If I was going to die, I wasn't going to ever be tortured again.

More bullets sprayed the area above my head, raining shards of jagged mirror down on my back. I crawled at warp speed to the other end of the bar, back near the hallway entrance to the stairs. Ben's running footsteps came my way. I reached the open end of the bar and dove out just in time to get a shot off at him as he hit the bar top where I'd jumped over. My hand went wild under the frantic recoil of the gun and caused my ribs to flare up in agony. His ankle exploded outward in a mist of red and he crashed into the bar's front, aiming at me over spilled drinks.

I lunged at the doorway and rolled into the hall just as the jamb was chewed up by a succession of rounds.

There was pain throughout my body the likes of which I'd never experienced. There wasn't a muscle or bone that didn't throb when I moved it. My entire face was so swollen now it hurt to blink.

Three people were in the hallway: the judge, Marshall's wife, and at the far end, standing halfway in another hallway, the bald man in the black suit from the basement.

"Obnoxious little shit," the judge said. "You think you can get out of here alive. We're going to rip you to scraps and let you die for eternity at the feet of Veles."

"Praise him," said Marshall's wife, her hair now in strings over her sweaty face.

I'm not cold blooded, but the gory stains on the judge's chin reminded me of how he'd eaten that girl downstairs with such glee that I knew he had to die. He was a judge for crying out loud, and would weasel out of any conviction they slapped against him. In fact, much as this knowledge and the thought of shooting unarmed people disturbed me, I would have capped all three of them right then and there to ensure proper justice if the man in the black suit hadn't nodded to me. Just like before. It was a slight nod of approval, strangely out of place, and I had no idea what it meant. It confused me for a second too long and gave Ben enough time to limp out of the doorway at the other end of the hall, gun raised.

With a roar of pure rage, he shot and hit Marshall's wife in the hip. She screamed and spun sideways like a Tilt-A-Whirl and I threw myself down the stairs, crashing into the wolf statue, leaving wide smears of my own blood on its cloven feet. Ben had the high ground now, an advantage that would allow him to blindly shoot down and probably hit me, so I bolted down the next flight of stairs and back onto the ground floor.

He didn't come after me right away, maybe stopping to check Marshall's wife, maybe afraid I would have a bead on him. There was too much screaming and commotion going on up there to be sure.

I needed to hide, to set up an ambush. Problem was, I couldn't leave, not with Victoria still strapped to the table in the Observation Room.

She'll be dead by the time you get back to her, Roger. You should have shot her and put her out of her misery. But then you never do save them, do you? You love to see them die. You're brutal and you love it.

Skinny Man. Leveling up my psychosis to the point I knew I was going to have to check myself into a funny farm if I lived. Dr. Marsh's calming exercises weren't going to do me any good right now; I was too scared and overcome with shaking, in too much pain and feeling lightheaded.

"You're fucking dead, kid! You hear me! You're a dead man!"

It was Ben, he was finally coming down the stairs, and with him the footfalls of the two other goons that were still functioning. I shambled my broken body back through the collection of rooms I'd traversed earlier, back to the dining room with its metal operating table now cleaned of that girl's blood, back to the hallways leading to the kitchens.

It was a game of cat and mouse and I couldn't think of a way to win. Ben would know shortcuts, passages, tricks to surprise me. I needed a plan.

I needed to hide.

Chapter 19

Back to my video game strategy: there are a collection of games with pretty good AI for the bad guys. In them, if you draw attention to yourself it'll bring out more enemies trying to kill you. I was in a real life video game now and had to think like a player. I only had to worry about three goons, but shooting one, if he was alone from the others, would give away my location, would draw the others. I had to ask myself just how badly I wanted to survive, and what I would do to ensure that. Could I be homicidal enough to take a man out silently with just my bare hands?

I'd done it to Skinny Man, had taken an ax to him in the end. It scared me to know I could do it again now. I'm not supposed to be okay with killing people, which is what I always told Dr. Marsh, but such thoughts don't faze me anymore, and it's why I knew therapy was never going to cure me.

I slinked into a small room with a large fish tank against the wall near the door and a television at the far end, some kind of recreational den. There was a stack of opened mail on an end table, and a letter opener on top of it all. I picked it up and switched the gun to my bum arm, just so I'd still have it if I needed it.

I hid down next to the fish tank, which was sitting on a big black cabinet, and waited. I felt my ribs and rubbed my fingers over the swollen lump there. For a few seconds I just listened, but I heard nothing, and I worried my predators had all gone back up to help Marshall resume dessert. The tank's filter bubbled noisily near my head, and I watched the fish swim lazily while trying to catch my breath and fight the pain overtaking my entire body. It was a saltwater tank, filled with bright clownfish, anemones, angelfish, and what looked like a tiny shark. It reminded me I had a beta fish back home. If I died, who would feed it?

Why did I even care?

Through the water I saw a shadow enter the room.

It stopped in the doorway, looking in. The lights came on, making my pupils hurt. I felt exposed, grit my teeth, wondering if he could see me through the tank somehow.

The goon stepped toward the couch, tentatively heading for a closet opposite me. He raised his gun and opened the door, ready to tear whoever was inside to ribbons.

I was out of my hiding spot in a flash, stepping onto the coffee table, jumping off, seeing the gunman spin around at the noise, a startled look in his eyes. He brought his gun up towards me.

I jammed the letter opener into the side of his neck, just below his ear. He went rigid, mouth falling open, gun trying to find me. I grabbed it and shoved it down, praying he didn't fire, pushed us both into the closet and let the door fall closed behind us, feeling him spasm against me. I twisted the letter opener and jammed it in further until the hilt was buried in deep, heard it scrape the low bones of his skull.

In the darkness the coats wrapped around us and he started to gurgle, his breath exhaling into my mouth and eyes. I let go of the letter opener and threw my good forearm against his Adam's apple and rubbed and pressed as hard as I could. His windpipe cracked and popped.

He slumped down, myself on top of him, both of us on our knees with me still trying to break everything in his throat. He was just about dead when bullets tore lighted holes in the door above my head and slammed into the back wall of the closet where'd we'd been standing a second ago. I spun around, testicles retreating up into my stomach. The closet door was wrenched open behind me, and without thinking I fired with my wounded arm. The sound of the gun shots made me temporarily deaf, but I saw the other goon fall backwards onto the coffee table, breaking it under his weight.

I screamed bloody murder, not because I'd just killed two men but because the pain in my arm was unearthly and I thought I was going to faint. So much so I dropped the gun and cried as I crawled back out into the room. Absentmindedly I leaned against the couch for a second and felt the baseball hat still on my head. Somehow that made me feel a little better and gave me strength. The struggle in the closet had opened up my gunshot wound even more and the blood was running hot and fast around the makeshift dressing. I tore the shirt bandage off, yanked an old sweater from the closet and wrapped it around the gaping hole, tied it as tight as I could, hoping to cut off the blood somehow. It was either that or pass out. Probably it did nothing but it gave me a psychological boost.

Ben would be coming now, would have heard the gun shots for sure. I needed a new hiding place stat.

Back in the hallway, I made a beeline toward the kitchen then thought twice about it. There was nowhere to hide in there except cupboards and the pantry and unless I wanted to go outside or downstairs—where'd I'd be lost and blind—I'd be trapped.

Instead I made my way back toward the dining room that had hosted the night's earlier scene of death and sorrow. It was a big room, again with two open entrances on either end, and would afford me the ability to retreat if I had to. I squatted down behind a couch, looked over it and gauged my surroundings. When I looked up I saw the giant chandelier above me and the wrap-around balcony with the bookshelves and struck onto an even better idea. I could go up there, throw one of the books from the bookshelves down to where I was now, attract Ben, and shoot him when he entered.

It was a better plan than anything I could think of at the moment.

So I was up there in a flash, using the stairs off the small sitting room, emerging through the upstairs guest room, and snagged a heavy leather-bound tome from the closest bookshelf. It was a copy of collected works by Raymond Chandler, probably some first edition that was worth more than my car, not that it mattered.

Aside from the guest room behind me, there was only one other room all the way around the balcony on the other side. I could see into its open door to another guest room, which at least gave me a heads up if anyone was coming at me that way.

The seconds ticked away as I listened silently for sounds of Ben nearing the room downstairs. I could still hear the faint sounds of yelling and shouting from the rooms above me, probably Marshall's wife screaming in pain. If only Ben had hit her in the head I'd at least have one less psycho to worry about.

For the first time I noticed all the weird shit in the room beneath me, all the little figures of one-eyed wolves and decorative daggers and headless women and scenes of sacrifices. Even the lampshades told stories of mothers and children being ripped to shreds by various demons. The grandfather clock in the corner had a swinging sword for a pendulum. The Persian rug wasn't Persian at all, but showed images of dogs and wolves and snakes wearing crowns and climbing trees. All of it looked very old and very expensive.

"*Antique Road Show* for the insane."

Just then I heard shuffling footsteps from somewhere below me, a low moan from a man trying to walk with a busted ankle.

"C'mon. C'mon. Just come on in," I said and raised the gun and waited, sweat dripping off my broken nose. When he didn't enter I threw the book down with all my might, hoping to make as loud a crash as I could. The book bounced off the medical table, flipped up and took out a small lamp before landing half in the fireplace.

It took only a second before it caught fire.

"Oh shit."

And then Ben was running in, stopping just below me so that I had to bend over the railing and aim at an almost backwards angle. He saw me at the same time and fired up. Bullets dug at the railing before me and I rolled back into the bookcase. Had I hit him at all?

"I'm going to kill you slow, kid."

Nope. Didn't hit him. "I've heard worse threats."

"It's not a threat."

I grabbed another book and hurled it toward the grandfather clock, merely hoping to distract him while I ran around the balcony trying to get a shot at him.

He was wise to my ruse and fired off a shot at me as soon as I got to the first corner, forcing me back toward the guest room. Two bullets came through the floor right next to me and I ducked into the guest room, realizing too late he was pushing me in the direction he wanted me to go.

I heard him coming up the stairs even now, knowing exactly where I was. He wouldn't even need to come in, just reach around the doorway and shoot me. I had to beat him to the punch, so I lay flat and stuck my gun out, saw his shoulder coming around the stairs at the bottom. Screaming, I fired and saw the bullets tear his shoulder to ground beef, saw the blood spit out like a geyser and hit the walls.

The gun locked as the last bullet was fired. His body fell forward onto the stairs.

Only it wasn't his body. It was the goon with the letter opener in his neck, still dead, positioned there by Ben before he'd entered the dining room.

Ben had tricked me. Lured me back where he wanted me and gotten me to empty my gun on a dead guy.

I scrambled to my feet. "Shit. Where the hell—"

It hit me out of nowhere, knowing exactly where he was coming from. I just knew it.

The other guest room.

Before I could even look out at the balcony I felt the floor shaking beneath me as he ran around toward me like a linebacker.

I panicked, grabbed the closest thing to me: a small nightstand on top of which sat a white clay lamp. The lamp crashed to the ground and shattered as I raced to the balcony, swinging the nightstand toward the massive hulk charging toward me. There was gunfire, and I felt the bullets explode into the top of the nightstand, waiting for them to pass through the wood and rip open my belly. My momentum kept me moving forward and Ben and I met in a crunch of flesh and furniture. I flew backwards to the guest room, Ben above me, stopping short as the nightstand's top and legs caught either side of the doorjamb and formed a barrier that knocked him back like a man bouncing off a rubber wall, his bullets firing into the ceiling. I grabbed my empty gun from the floor and leapt over the nightstand at him as he righted himself, brought the gun down like a hammer on his head, trying to nail something invisible to his brain. He fired again, killing the books beside me and sending literary confetti into the air around us to join the smoke drifting toward the chandelier.

Smoke?

I smelled it but couldn't care less. Ben was going to kill me unless I killed him first. So I hit him again in the head, caught him square in the eye as he punched out and found my chest, tossing me into the railing like I was made of straw.

Beneath me I saw flames.

Ben came at me again but I ducked and he swooned, dizzy from the head trauma, and for a second fell against the railing beside me, hands on the banister to hold himself up, head and torso leaning over it as he waited for his vision to clear.

It was all I needed.

I threw my arm around his waist and lifted with all my might, catching an elbow in my throat which made me scream so loud I thought my own ears would bleed, but I heaved until my back was twisted in agony and felt him start to go over. I thought of Victoria upstairs and what Marshall might be doing to her, thought of how this bastard Ben had brought her up there and chained her down.

I thought of Jamie, and how I hadn't been able to save her.

Ben's body reached its fulcrum point and started to tip. In his frantic struggle to stay upright he fired at the ground below and tried to push back from the railing. But I pushed harder than I've ever pushed before and felt his weight lift off of me as he went over.

He fell to the ground below, his back hitting one of the chairs around the medical table. Funny thing is he stood up right away, screaming, holding his backbone, and then staggered forward a few steps before falling into the tiny fire on the rug that had once been Philip Marlowe's life story.

Then he went still, groaning. "Marshall," he said. I think it hurt him too much to even talk.

His pant legs caught fire.

"Marshall. I can't . . ."

The flames were crawling up to his knees, as well as across the rug to the couch. He couldn't move, most likely had broken a few vertebrae on the chair, which was now splintered. He was burning, and the sad thing is it wasn't even the first time I'd seen someone burn to death.

The fire crawled up faster than I would have expected, perhaps aided by something in Ben's cheap suit. I caught a glimpse of white calf melting away to red goo, saw him start twitching, then shaking, trying to slither away, but impeded by whatever had become of his skeletal system.

Finally he screamed as the fire reached his groin and licked out around the sides of him on the rug. Everything below me was crackling and popping, including Ben's flesh.

And then . . . agony, pain, fire in my head, white light and a final image of my feet covered in my own blood.

I fainted.

Chapter 20

I wasn't out very long, not long enough to remember anything I might have dreamed of, because when I woke up in a sitting position against the bookcase, I could still see Ben's head in one piece.

And no doubt everyone in the house could hear him screaming.

"No! NO!" followed by a bunch of bloodcurdling screeches that should have cracked any glass in their vicinity.

Figured I was out only a few seconds, my body recharging form the exertion I'd forced on it getting Ben over the railing. There were no new bullet holes anywhere in me that I could see or feel, which had been my first concern. Somehow that damn nightstand had saved me and if I ever found out who made the thing I'd buy twenty of them.

Victoria, I thought.

Ben had taken his gun down to the dining room with him, but I wasn't about to play firefighter trying to get it. As much as I wanted it, I couldn't waste time wading through the flames for it. I'd have to make do with an empty one and hope my acting skills were better than my fighting skills. Before I left back through the guest room I finally saw Ben's hair catch on fire.

His screams were shrill.

I leapt over Mr. Letter Opener and raced back toward the main stairs, aware now the smoke from the dining room was pluming out in thick black clouds. With all the art and antiques Marshall had collected I expected a fire sprinkling system to kick in, but there wasn't one.

When I got back up to the Observation Room I simply walked in gun raised, and stopped.

They were all huddled against the floor-to-ceiling windows, bent over Marshall's wife, who was still cursing in pain.

Marshall turned at my approach and stood up. Some others

stood up beside him. "Roger, you've come back to us."

"Shut up! Just shut up and don't fucking move!"

"Are you going to shoot us? Right here? Just put an end to us in cold blood?"

"He can't get all of us, Marshall," said Judge Coates, "Not if we rush him."

I stabbed the gun forward. "You go first, asshole. Take a step and I put the first bullet in your head."

The judge stopped, stood still, looking to Marshall for instructions.

I backed up to the medical table, which was still flipped over. A puddle of blood had formed around it, already turning tacky on the hardwood floor. Victoria's whimpers drifted out from underneath, and I watched her hands and feet moving as if she were trying to walk away somewhere.

"Hang on," I said, and bent down. Now here's where I got scared, because I had one good arm, and that was holding the gun. But I needed to flip the table over and free Victoria. "It's me, Roger. Just hang on."

I think she cried a little louder at my voice but I can't be sure.

"You, old bitch, get over here. Now!" I said.

The white-haired lady couldn't care less about what I'd called her, and to prove she wasn't afraid she didn't move.

"I said get over here."

"You little brat. Don't you realize if you kill me I am just made stronger. I am loyal to Veles and he will send me back to eat your girlie soul."

I'd heard that damn name, Veles, so many times tonight, but still had no idea who they were talking about, and right then I didn't care.

"For people who aren't afraid to die you spend a lot of time eating humans to stay young. But I'm in no mood to debate. If you don't move now I'm gonna SHOOT YOU IN THE FUCKING FACE!"

Marshall touched her shoulder, keeping his eyes on me. "Go ahead, Belle, I won't let him hurt you."

"Marshall I don't want—"

"Belle! Move!" Marshall's eyes narrowed into devilish little slits. He was not amused by any of this.

Belle waddled her cannibalistic fat ass over toward me with her lips curled in a snarl.

I gestured down at Victoria. "Undo her cuffs, flip the table off her."

"I don't have the key."

"Who does?"

"How should I know? I'm not hosting tonight."

Marshall pulled the key from his breast pocket and held it up. "I have it here. But you do realize it is fruitless to unbind her. You'll have to carry her and unless you shoot us . . ." His eyes flicked to the floor between us, to the two dead goons lying in a heap of un-natural muscles and oversized bones. I saw what he saw: the gun squished between them.

It was just what I needed to have the upperhand. I moved forward and wrenched it free, keeping my gun on Marshall the whole time. "Throw the key to Broom Hilda. Now!" I dropped my un-loaded gun and aimed the new one at him, and for a moment I saw him questioning the move. Thing is, he was either kicking himself for not realizing my first gun was empty, or he knew this one was. It really didn't matter either way: if he charged and this gun was empty, I was going to have to fight him man-to-man regardless.

Belle attempted to catch the key, dropped it, but then stopped and picked it up and began unlocking Victoria.

"Faster," I said. Smoke meandered into the room, and the guests were starting to both notice it and smell it. "Flip the table off of her. Now! Hurry!"

The old lady heaved as she struggled to move the heavy med-ical table, slowly revealing Victoria, who was still on her stomach, lying in her own blood.

I bent down and whispered in her ear: "Victoria, it's Roger, can you hear me?"

She whimpered and moaned. Could have been in response to my voice or could just have been in response to the awkward pain she was in.

"I'm still here and I'm getting you out, but I need you to stand. C'mon, take my shoulder. That's it."

She started crying, refusing to look at me, but she reached up and found my right shoulder, pulled herself up off the floor. I did my best to help her up without taking my gun off the Crazy Clan. Immediately I realized that Marshall was dead right, that carrying Victoria was going to be a pain in the ass.

Still, I managed to get her up and fought back a gasp at what I saw. She was completely red with blood so thick it looked like she'd gone swimming in molasses. Deep cuts were gouged in her flesh, in her belly, her thighs, her breasts. She was going to need plenty of stitches and possible skin grafts to fix it all. Worst of all was the giant slice in her left cheek, which was open from the back of her jaw to her lips. It reminded me of Tooth after Skinny Man had wrapped razor wire around his head. You're not supposed to see someone's face like that, so exposed and skeletal. If they could fix it the scar would leave her looking like the Joker.

I grabbed the nearest covering I could find—the tablecloth that had been folded up and put on a small chair—wrapped it around her like a toga. Blood seeped through it before I could even tie it, which wasn't easy with my injuries.

If I'd been at the other end of the room staring at us, I'm sure I would have been shocked we were even still mobile. Gun shot, stabbed, beaten, cut, bleeding out, purple and black all over.

"We have to go, just walk the best you can. And you" –I pointed the gun at Belle—"back up to your friends there. Go!"

"We're going to find you and kill you," she said, so I kicked her in the back and sent her flying toward the others. She screamed and landed on her hip and I prayed that I'd broken it. Cite me for elderly abuse if you want, the bitch had it coming.

Together, Victoria and I backed up slowly toward the doorway, then to the stairs, keeping my gun trained on Marshall and his friends.

I yelled at Marshall through the doorway. "If you take one step from there I will shoot you."

"You could shoot us now. Your weakness will only bring us to you faster."

I could *shoot now*, I thought, but something stopped me. Maybe it was the look in Victoria's eyes, the way she stared into the distance as if something had died inside of her and been replaced by a darkness too vast to understand. Maybe it was the way I wanted something more appropriate for these lunatics. Maybe it was the way I was scared of how much I wanted to kill them.

Yeah, it was all of that.

Smoke danced up the stairwell and started to cloud my vision. Victoria coughed and clutched me tighter.

I looked at her, put my chin on her bare shoulder and brushed my nose against her bloody cheek. "I'm not afraid of him anymore."

She had no idea what I meant, and I had no idea why I said it. I just knew that this time, I wasn't going to let her die first.

We hurried down the steps as fast as we could go. When we got to the ground floor, flames were already licking out of the dining room. The chaise lounge was on fire, and one hallway was cut off with thick, black smoke.

"This way," I said, shuttling her toward the small kitchen. She limped as we walked, shuddering with each step. For the first time, I couldn't feel my left arm at all. It reminded me of what it feels like to wake up after sleeping on it too long. You can see it, but you can't move it or even sense it. Down one of the labyrinthine hallways I saw some of the staff running about. I also saw the bald-headed man looking at me, before he stepped out of view and disappeared.

The temperature in the house was rising, and I felt like we were walking through an oven. Things sizzled around us, and I caught sight of flames in other rooms now. The fire was spreading fast, fueling itself on old dry rugs, wooden antiques, scores of furniture and art. The wide open rooms gave it plenty of oxygen, enough that it was jumping from room to room like it was being shot from a flamethrower.

"Almost there." Through the smoke, I saw the entrance to the kitchen in front of us. "Just keep walking. We're almost—"

Then the kitchen exploded.

A wall of flame came at us like a tidal wave, the heat so intense the hairs on my good arm burned off. Instinctively, I threw myself over Victoria as we dove to the ground. The flames passed over us and lit up the ceiling above, black smoke shrouding us as if we were underwater. My bare torso stung with the heat and I prayed I didn't get third-degree burns.

It was all I could do to roll us into the nearest hallway, choking and coughing, gasping for any bit of air we could find like fish on a beach.

"Gas stoves," I said, "don't do well in fires."

In the darkness I saw a shadowy door handle and reached up for it. My eyes stung, my lungs burned, I thought we would melt away to nothing. When I opened the door, there were stairs going down.

"This way. C'mon."

We crawled toward the stairs, went down them on our asses, trying to stay as low as we could. The air cooled ever so slightly and finally we were out of the smoke.

Burning holes in the floor above us provided enough light to see we were in the basement. Glowing embers fell down like tiny falling stars. They'd soon catch something on fire around us but for now the fire remained above us. I could see this wasn't the same area as before but it was similar, with more wolf statues and old furniture draped in coverings. The only way out I knew of from down here was through the tunnel.

"Roger." She said my name with a quivering voice. It could have meant a million different things. Could have been out of fear, or resignation, or perhaps just sudden realization of where she was.

"I'm here. Breathe through the cloth, it'll filter the air."

She did as I told her, her brain somehow knowing enough to follow my command.

We weaved among the statues, trying to get a bearing. There was a door to my right. I opened it and emerged in a larger room, also glowing from the fire above. This room was familiar, the one you emerged in from the stairs in the kitchen.

"This way. I know where we are."

We went around more statues, ducking out of the way of falling tinder, hearing the rush of air above us as it was eaten by the fire. The house above us roared like an angry dragon awakened from thousands of years of sleep.

The doorway to the tunnel was just ahead of us, and my heart leapt. We were going to make it.

And then they all stepped out from the shadows.

Wolves.

Wolves walking on their hind legs. Each one carrying something sharp: an ax, a spear, a sword, a machete, even scissors.

The creatures formed a half moon in front of us, blocking our exit, laughing in a macabre song of death.

"We warned you to kill us upstairs, boy."

That voice. I knew it.

"Judge Coates."

Before I could say any more there was an order given. It came from Marshall, the wolfman standing in the center of the blockade. "Kill him."

Chapter 21

The arc of wolves drew closer, illuminated under small fiery holes in the ceiling; they each wore masks. If you could call them masks. They were real wolf heads, at least they looked real, hollowed out and fashioned to fit snugly on the top of one's head. Every one had had its eyes removed and replaced with an eyeball in the center of the head.

I could tell who was who from their voices and clothing, but still the effect was hellish. These people were beyond nuts. Victoria shook her head no but could not find her voice.

I knew now I'd have to kill them to get by. I wasn't going to go out like this nor was I going to let them touch Victoria. I raised my gun and fired. A single bullet shot out and plugged a hole in Marshall's chest. He stopped advancing for a second, then resumed his walk.

"Praise Veles," he said.

I couldn't tell if he was bleeding or not. He looked hurt, but how he was still walking was beyond me. Then again here I was with a bullet hole in my arm and I was moving okay. Maybe he had a protective vest on. Maybe he was lucky and the bullet missed his major organs.

He just kept coming.

"Praise Veles," they all chanted in unison, raising their weapons over their heads.

I squeezed the trigger again and the gun went *click*.

A choir of laughs rose above the roaring flames in the house above. Had Marshall somehow known there was only one bullet in the gun? Or did they all just not care in light of letting us escape and facing the idea I'd get their story out.

"Stay back! I'll kill you, I swear."

"My boy," Marshall laughed. "It is our hour, not yours. You

made the worst mistake of your life coming here. Bullets cannot stop us. Nothing can."

I stepped in front of Victoria, surrounded on the sides by wolf statues, watching the shimmering silhouettes of the cannibals advancing forward, wondering if we could run back to the kitchen stairs, wondering how we were going to get out from underneath the burning house.

And then I heard the voice. The voice I hear a lot that makes me realize I am crazy, that I need a padded room. The voice I have heard for ten years, even while on my meds, even when I hit my own head to make it go away and appear normal in public.

It's the voice that scares me even more than Skinny Man's, because unlike Skinny Man's, I can *feel* it. And it feels so real that I secretly long for it.

Tooth.

It was unmistakable, even though it was probably just me misinterpreting the roaring fire above, shouting in my ear with a sense of urgency that forced me to move before I could even think. "This way! Jump!"

I lunged sideways, bodychecking Victoria in front of me, both of us crashing to the floor at the base of a statue. I looked back just in time to see the entire ceiling fall in a flaming circle the diameter of a redwood tree, crushing the group of masked crazies beneath it. Above me the giant hole looked up into some kind of wood-paneled room, totally engulfed in fire.

"Up. Let's go." I grabbed Victoria and helped her to her feet. Together we raced over the burning circle of floor, through the flames, vaguely hearing the cries of the people underneath it. It wobbled and teetered as we crossed it, crushing Marshall and his followers' bones.

We were through the door to the tunnel just as they all started screaming. When I shut the door, I glanced through the window and saw arms and legs sticking out from under the fallen floor on the other side, all of them on fire. I watched them for a second, seeing their flesh roasting and turning black.

In the distance of the orange basement, there was an outline of someone walking away. "Tooth?" I whispered.

Now Victoria was screaming, a desperate plea that cut through my trance. She was staring at the cages, staring at Bob's drugged up, dickless, unconscious body in the middle of the dirt.

It was time to go.

Before I raced to her, I looked back through the door one last time, saw Marshall's unmasked head emerge from under the boards. His hair was on fire.

I locked the door.

"Victoria," I shouted as I grabbed her. She saw my face, my broken and swollen face, and reached up to touch it, suddenly stopping her screams. "Step over. Don't touch him. Let him stay here and fry."

We stepped over Bob and made our way down the exit tunnel, found the ladder leading up to the shed. I went up first, checking for the lock, which was still secured. It was a simple latch that flipped open, and once I did that I scrambled back down and shoved Victoria up. "Climb. Hurry."

She did, and I followed.

We emerged in the shed, and walked out on to the backyard lawn. We stopped for a moment and sucked in clean air. Before us, the house was a mountain of flame, reaching up toward the dark sky above us. Parts of it had already caved in.

As we made our way down past the carport, then down the driveway, keeping ourselves shielded with cars and trees and other barriers, I thought I could still hear the people screaming in the basement. But then, I thought I'd seen and heard a lot in that basement. But you know why at this point.

My car was still where I'd left it, the keys still on the seat. I'd done that on purpose to have a quick getaway. One thing I learned from that summer in Skinny Man's basement was to be proactive. I hadn't been about to give up or lose my keys in a fight.

The car started without a problem. In the passenger seat, Victoria put her head against the side window and sobbed. I stared at the streaks of blood she left on the glass, leaned over and touched her shoulder. The tablecloth draped around her was black and had burn holes in it. The rest was covered in dirt and blood.

"Victoria. We're safe now."

She turned and looked at me, tears welling in her eyes. Her breath grew shallower and she was shaking. Her teeth showed through the slice in her cheek. "Gabe."

It was the last thing she said before she put her head back against the glass and retreated inside of herself.

She was alive, though. I hadn't let them kill her first. This time, the girl didn't die.

I drove for many minutes, lost in the back roads but unconcerned about having no bearings, just happy to be free. There are no words to describe the pain I felt, both physically and emotionally, as I did my best to steer us away from the hell we'd just escaped. Looking at Victoria, my heart hurt as much as my face and arm.

The trees soon gave way to a main road lined with cafes and real estate offices. It wasn't a big road, nor very long, but it was civilized, and I heaved a sigh of relief. Above us in the sky, the moon swam out from behind the clouds, just enough to give me a little extra light.

Then my eyes sank down to my knees, fatigue and blood loss finally forcing me against the ropes for their final takedown.

My foot slid off the gas pedal. The car drifted forward, slowing, turning, and finally crashing through the front window of a bakery.

All I remember before I passed out was: *it smells like Sunday morning*.

Chapter 22

Where to begin?

I guess with the hospital.

I woke up there, bandaged, splinted, with IVs feeding me a kind of supplement that made me itch. I saw faces hovering above me, but none that I recognized. A lot of them were male, and most had sunglasses on.

"Roger? Can you hear me?"

A man in a dark gray suit bent over me. He had a bushy mustache and his breath stank of coffee.

"Mmm," I said.

On the other side of the bed a man in a white coat leaned over. "Roger, I'm Doctor Lipski. Do you remember me?"

I shook my head no. Realization was coming back to me though, little by little, and I had vague memories of being put in an ambulance, then wheeled through some white hallways, then having an oxygen masked placed over my face. Or maybe it wasn't oxygen, because I had no memory whatsoever from then 'til now.

"Roger, you're lucky to be alive." Dr. Lipski sat down, put his arm on my own. "You're in St. Mercy Hospital. You've been out for a couple of days. These men here are detectives, and they need to ask you some questions. But your health takes precedence over their interrogation so I'm here to stop it if you can't talk any more. And before I can even let them start I need to check some vitals on you, okay?"

His words registered but had little meaning to me. Suddenly my only thought was of Victoria. I didn't even know why I was thinking of her, just that I needed to know if she was okay.

I rolled my head sideways, felt a wave of nausea crash over me, but somehow managed to fight it down. "Victoria?"

"She's in another room."

"I don't want him to see her," said Mr. Mustache. "Not until we've established some facts."

"Definitely not until he answers some questions," said one of the other detectives. "And tell them to turn the TV off across the hall."

I wouldn't have even noticed the news story coming out of the room across the way if he hadn't said that. But I caught the last little bit of some reporter's chattering before the TV went off: ". . . say they have a suspect in the case of Marshall Aldrich's mansion fire."

And so it began. The questioning, the cross examinations, the detectives coming back hour after hour for two whole days, as they tried to make sense of what I'd done.

"I didn't let him kill her," I repeated. I'd been saying this a lot.

"But you shot those men?"

"They had to die."

"You killed nineteen people, Roger. I'm just not following this story."

"They were wolves. They ate people."

"You're referring to some of the statues?"

"Ugly statues. Probably worth millions." This from one of the other detectives.

"No," I said. "Marshall."

I was getting frustrated but was having a hard time expressing it since the morphine had me in a daze.

"What did you do to Victoria, Roger? She keeps saying your name. Did you rape her? Did you do that to her. Her insides are ruined, do you know that?"

"Told you. Saved her. Not afraid anymore."

"I'm afraid I'm going to have to ask you to leave," said the doctor.

"We're not done, doc."

"You are now. I told you. Twenty minutes at a time. Come back later. He needs to rest."

And that was how it went until the third day when Victoria began to speak. I'll just cut to the chase here.

She woke up to her parents, an aunt and uncle and cousin. A whole extended family had come to see her. The detectives were there as well. The doctors had sewn up her fissure, taken skin from her buttocks to cover up some of the wounds. Like me, she had superficial burns on her body. The scar on her cheek was thick, and the doctors told her she'd need lots of plastic surgery to get it back to something that wouldn't scare little kids.

She asked about Gabe a lot, and I heard her crying the night they told her he was dead. I'd already told her of course, but she'd retreated so far inside her own mind that she'd forgotten. She cried for so long. If anyone in this world ever tells you love is not real, make them listen to someone crying like that. It was the sound of someone's soul dying.

At some point she recounted her story. There were holes of course, but enough to begin to put the pieces together. It took about another week for forensics to start corroborating. Leslie came out of the woodwork as well. He'd called the cops about Gabe and Walt and they'd been drilling him ever since. When word got out I was in the hospital they brought him there to confirm everything. I heard him in the hallway with the detectives. From what I could make out he repeated for the umpteenth time the story about Walt and the incident at the house on his road. It all matched up with Victoria's account. Of course I corroborated as well. Leslie was pretty much a hero.

The doctor asked me if I wanted to call my family. Apparently the detectives had gotten him to hold off on that until they'd had time to talk to me. I told him to call them but tell them I was okay and not to fly out. I mean, it's not like they weren't going to read about this soon enough. Once my name got out and that I was in-volved in another murder—murder spree, rather—all those web-sites and magazines that had reported on me in the past were going to have a field day.

But get this: when the detectives finally came back to my room, they apologized. They actually said they were sorry, and congratu-lated me.

"But," Mustache said, "don't get us wrong. We're still investi-gating, and if any of this starts to smell like lies we're gonna have you behind bars faster than you can think. I am still finding it hard to think Marshall Aldrich and Winston Coates and all these others did everything you say they did."

"Where's my car?" It was all I could think of right then.

"In holding." The detective waited a moment and then ran his hand through his hair. I could see he was exhausted from trying to make sense of all this. "I'll get it for you. But remember what I said."

Then I was alone for a while, just me and my thoughts, and all I could think of was that the detectives would never know the half of it. How many others had the cannibals eaten? How many others had been kidnapped and raped? Where had the bodies been taken? Marshall wasn't Skinny Man, he wouldn't bury them in the backyard; he'd get rid of them for good somehow. And I hadn't heard anything about the cages and tunnels. Maybe the house had fallen in on it and burned it all.

Except the wolf statues. The detectives had mentioned them.

"Praise Veles," I whispered, wondering just what the hell had really been taking place in that mansion. "Eat shit, Veles. I beat you."

When I could walk again, I found myself in Victoria's room. There was a uniformed officer outside the door who gave me a funny look when I passed by. Pride, contempt, I dunno, I couldn't tell.

Her parents were in there sitting next to the bed, her father looking stoic, her mother looking like she'd just come back from a war—eyes red, skin pasty, her hands constantly wringing themselves. I understood it, maybe more than anyone. No one wants to see their child like this.

"You're Roger?" her father asked.

I nodded. I was back to that again. Just nodding and hoping I didn't have to answer questions.

Her mother walked up to me, studied my face. The seconds ticked away as she looked for something inside of me. "Thank you," she said.

I nodded again.

Victoria's parents were gracious enough to give me a moment of privacy with her, said they were going to go down to the cafeteria and get some food. I sat in the chair beside her bed, tried hard to see her as the girl I'd fallen for, the spritely girl from the gallery. She looked different, had lost weight, was bandaged up pretty good. Part of her hair had been shaved off to sew in stitches; the scar on her cheek was under a dressing coated in a mustardy stain. I hoped it was just iodine or some other type of antibacterial agent.

I reached out and took her hand. It was cold.

She opened her eyes and looked at me.

"Hi," I said.

The corners of her mouth turned up slowly. It wasn't much of a smile, maybe all she could muster, but it was enough for me. Finally, her fingers closed on my hand. I put my head down on her chest and smelled the hospital gown, listened to her heartbeat. For some reason I just wanted to know she was still alive. I wanted to hear the life inside of her, to know that it was going to continue. I wanted to kiss her, but not the way I had wanted to in the past, not in a passionate way. I just wanted to let her know I cared. Her other hand came up and stroked my hair. Her hands were delicate. Her chest rose and fell in a way that felt like I was drifting on a calm sea.

I knew right then as I looked at her, as I felt the heat of her body against my ear, that she would never be the same. Something was long dead in her now.

I knew the feeling.

I still know the feeling.

I had saved her, but only part of her. I had still let part of her die.

We stayed like that for a while, holding hands, my head on her chest, cherishing every heartbeat, until her parents came back in.

It must have looked a little weird but they didn't say anything. I left without another word.

Two days later I was allowed to go home.

But as with everything in my life, I was to find that things were not going to be okay. In fact, things were about to get a whole lot worse.

Chapter 23

The hospital kept my clothes in a pile in the closet near the bathroom. My jeans were burned and stained beyond recognition, my white sneakers now entirely black. The Red Sox cap was there, burned in places and ripped in others. It had looked decrepit before I'd broken into Marshall's place; now it looked like it had been dug out of a trash heap.

My *Ghost in the* Shell shirt was missing. I had torn it off after stabbing one of the goons. It was no doubt a small pile of ashes near a charred wolf statue somewhere. The hospital, in all their sterile and officious graciousness, gave me a flannel button-down that was obviously pulled from the used overstock bins at Goodwill. It was too tight around my neck, but at least it covered up my fish white arms and belly.

My car's hood was dented, but beyond that was in pretty good shape. It started right up when I put the key in.

The drive home was somber. I listened to the news but heard nothing about the incidents at the Aldrich manor. Victoria was still in the hospital and would be for many days to come. She had more counselors than a pothead has places to hide weed. I hadn't gone back to see her after our little meeting, nor would I ever. In the years that followed I thought about her often, but I never bothered to pick up the phone. Other things became more important, and I rarely had the time to chit-chat.

When I got home I tore the constricting shirt off and tossed it right in the trash, put on my favorite Will Eisner collectable t-shirt. I spent some time staring at myself in the mirror, admiring my slanted nose. My eyes were still swollen and black, and my arm was in both a cast and a sling.

"You're a looker, hot stuff. Can't understand why the girls avoid you. Oh wait, because they all end up dead when they hang out with you."

My beta fish was still swimming in its tiny bowl of a world. It was lucky, because if I'd been killed no one would have come to feed it. I gave it some food, let it eat, and then walked across the hall to the apartment opposite me. A tiny Korean woman answered, wiping her hands on a food-stained apron.

"Hi, I'm Roger. I live . . . um . . . there." I pointed to my apartment.

"I know you," she said in perfect English. "I've seen you come and go. Do you need something?"

Her accent surprised me, because I'd never heard her speak but had, on numerous occasions, heard her yell at her children in Korean.

"What do you want?" she pressed, staring at my black eyes with appropriate suspicion.

I held up the fishbowl with my shiny blue pet inside. "I saw you have kids. I thought they might like this. I'm not meant to have it. She needs someone who will feed her every day, change her water once in a while. That sort of thing."

"We already have a cat and a Chihuahua."

"You're allowed to have cats? They told me . . ." I couldn't finish the thought because she was staring at my bandages and making me uncomfortable. "Forget it. I just want to find the fish a good home. Would your kids take care of it if I gave it to them?"

As if on cue, one of the children, a girl of perhaps seven, appeared beneath her mother's arm.

"I'll feed her!" she said. "Can I, Mom, can I?"

I held up the small shaker of fish food. "This should last at least a year. Just put the bowl where the cat can't get it, okay?"

The little girl nodded emphatically and did her best big doe-eyed impression for her mom.

The woman reluctantly took the fishbowl and said something in Korean that looked like an admonishment to her offspring. Probably something along the lines of, "This is your fish now, kid, and if you mess up and it dies then you won't get any more."

The little girl thanked me about a million times and I somehow knew she'd take good care of it.

Back in my apartment, I checked my email, saw I had nothing

but spam and online bill payments due.

Wait, there was also a message from Dr. Marsh. I opened it:

Roger, tried calling but got no answer. I really think you should come in. I heard about what happened on the news. I think you need to talk about all of this. I'm very afraid this is going to set our work back. I also would like to report on your prescriptions and start you on some others. We can discuss it when we meet. Please call me at your earliest convenience.

Sincerely,
Gail Marsh, Ph.D.

"Not very likely." I deleted the email. While I did need to get back on my meds, I wasn't about to go back to Dr. Marsh's office and let her pick my brain about what happened with Victoria. It was over and done with and I wanted it to stay that way.

Since crashing my car into the bakery window, I hadn't heard any voices in my head. I hadn't seen any boogey men hiding in the shadows. I hadn't had a conversation with a ghost. I probably *did* need to get back on meds, but right now I was going with this new wave of silence.

I turned around and found a man standing behind me. In my apartment. "Who the hell are you? How'd you get in? How'd you—"

Ice ran down my veins as I recognized the bald-headed man from Aldritch's mansion. "You."

I raced to my bookshelf to grab the heavy Lord of the Rings bookend I keep there, intent on throwing it at him or bludgeoning him with it, but he put up his hand and said, "Relax, Roger, I just want to talk to you. I'm not here to hurt you."

"Bullshit. I saw you in the house. You were with those freaks."

"No. I wasn't. I was there for something else. I was not associated with anyone in the house."

I couldn't believe it. I wanted to scream. I thought this was done with. Had more of those damn cannibals come to find me and kill me?

"I'm not afraid of you," I said.

"I know you're not afraid, that's why I'm here. My name is James Peter Fountain. I have come to offer you something. Can you please put down the . . . what is that? It's got rather a sharp spire on top."

"Cast iron miniature replica of Minas Tirith. Came with the limited edition DVDs."

"Yes, well, can you place it back on the shelf? I don't feel like getting stabbed by a small . . . whatever that is."

I put it back and stood against my wall. James Peter Fountain drew closer and motioned for me to sit. So I did, ready to pounce at a moment's notice. I'm not sure why I was even granting him an audience. If he was in fact associated with Marshall he probably had a machete under his suit.

"You always use three names?"

He smiled. "No, of course not. I'm merely giving you a bit of extra information to help you make sense of things. I was named after the two monks who raised me in the monastery where I grew up in Poland. I know little of my origins other than I had been abandoned by my mother when I was very young, left outside the monastery alongside the small fountain in the front. Hence the name."

For the first time I noticed the crucifix hanging around his neck. It was small and gold and looked a lot like the one I had in my car.

"You're a priest or something?"

"No. Not at all. Though I am . . . funded . . . by many organizations with religious influence. It's sort of a don't-ask-don't-tell policy. I wear this because I believe there is a higher power. Sort of came with my upbringing."

"So what are you offering?"

"An opportunity. But first I need to explain some things to you."

"Like what you were doing at that mansion," I said.

"I was there, in fact, to find you."

"I don't follow."

"I have been watching you for some time, Roger. Well, rather, my people have been watching you."

"You have people?"

"Here and there."

"Sounds pretty clandestine."

"I run a sort of agency, but I will get to that. I was at Marshall Aldritch's house because I was following you. I had been following you all day."

"If you were in that house and saw what was happening why didn't you do something? Call the cops, help Victoria escape. Are you telling me you stood by and watched all of that?"

His expression barely changed, but there was a hint of regret. It didn't stop the fact that I wanted to punch him square in the face.

"I had to," he said. "I had to see what you could do."

"What's that mean? You wanted to watch me end up like this." I raised my broken arm to punctuate my point.

"It was not easy. And before you ask me about the other girl, I was not in the house yet when that happened. I would have changed my plans and helped her. But I arrived too late. At that point I decided to let things play out because I had to know."

"Had to know what?"

"How you would survive."

I almost laughed. "Survive? Victoria is ruined. I almost died."

"But you didn't. And it confirmed my suspicions. Roger, I came to find you to tell you that you have a gift. An amazing gift."

"I'm about two seconds away from hitting you with that spire."

"Roger, I first became aware of you after reading about your incident with a mad man in New Hampshire. It sparked my interest. That's how it always starts. I find clues here and there, do more research based on that. I delved further into your story and saw signs that no one else was seeing. Signs about you. Have you ever noticed how things tend to work in your favor? How you manage to survive situations most people would never make it out of? I believe you were born with a power, a power that is hard to define. You're very lucky, Roger."

I pointed to my face. "You call this luck."

"I call it destiny. I think you were put on this earth to find yourself in the exact situations you've survived."

"What, you're telling me I was born to bleed?"

"I think that's rather a strong and suggestive way of putting it, but for lack of a better argument . . . yes. I think you were born to help. And as such, you have been given a bit more of a chance than others. It's not much of a power, I admit, but it's a very special one. Fate works in your favor."

"That's crap. I am not meant to do anything. I got out of those situations because psychos are crazy and don't think things through."

"Roger, my organization is made for people like you. I could use your help. There are others like you. Gifted, strong-willed, prone to surviving horrors that make the world sick as a whole. I want to offer you a place with my company."

"Okay, Professor X, I think it's time I call the cops."

He withdrew a gun from a shoulder holster and pointed it to my side. It had a silencer on it. "There are unspeakable horrors in this world, Roger, that the law cannot eradicate. The law has rules to follow, and so many bad men know how to exploit those laws. That's where my team comes in. What you saw in Marshall Aldritch's house was just the tip of the iceberg. You saw how far the police got with them. Nowhere. It gets worse. I've seen babies torn from their mother's wombs and eaten alive by grown men. I've seen women buried up to their heads in sand and left to die at the teeth of rats."

"Okay, enough. Is this the last thing I get to hear before you shoot me? I really just don't care anymore."

"Roger, you were put on this earth to stop these things. They will find you whether you like it or not, but at least with me, I can prepare you."

"Okay, this is ridiculous, and I'm done with this." I started to rise.

He fired the gun. The bullet hit the cushion next to me.

I froze, waiting for the next one to hit my chest.

"Roger," he continued, "do you ever feel like you can commune with the dead?"

"I'm crazy, don't you know that? I hear and see all sorts of things."

"But it tends to work in your favor, correct?"

My eyes didn't leave the gun. "You saying Tooth is really talking to me from the great beyond?"

"Of course not. I have no proof to explain such a thing. I merely ask the question. Even if his voice is just a figment of your imagination, does it not still help you? Some of my people suffer the same affliction."

"Tooth is dead. I went crazy long ago and can't get him out of my head. Dr. Marsh explained all this to me. It's post-traumatic—"

He fired the gun again. The bullet hit the cushion on the other side of me.

I found myself breathing in gulps now.

"Roger, there are horrors in this world that only you can stop. You have an unexplainable gift that allows you to survive. Trust me when I say I am one of the good guys."

I grit my teeth. "You're a crackpot."

He pointed the gun at my chest and pulled the trigger.

Click.

I flinched, squinted my eyes, felt my heart skip a beat, waiting for another shot.

"Look, Roger."

I looked. He slid the clip out of the gun and showed it to me.

"It's a full clip," he said. "The gun works well enough. It just fired twice without a problem. Yet it just misfired when I pointed it at you." I didn't know what to say. This was all beyond nuts.

"Not all that extraordinary," he said. "Guns misfire more often than people think."

"Yeah, I've had my fair share lately."

"Yes, I know."

"And sometimes they hit me." I motioned to my arm.

"Sometimes, yes. But you are alive, and here my gun has jammed. This time."

"So what are you saying? You saying that I can't be killed?"

He chuckled and put the gun away. I thought about rushing him but had to admit what just happened had me weirded out. I wanted to find some sense in it. I wanted to find some sense in why Skinny Man had never rolled my numbers, why that ceiling had fallen on the cannibals, why Mr. Budweiser's gun had seized on him in the shed.

James Peter Fountain smoothed his suit. "I dare think if I were to fire it again the bullet would go through your heart and you'd be dead in seconds. No, the point here is not to tempt fate, but point out that it tends to work in your favor more than the average person. That misfire would have given you enough time to attack me. But if you failed to attack, and I really was here to kill you, I think you would be quite dead."

Those words brought me back to reality. "You just fucking shot at me to prove a point! What the flying fuck!"

"But you're alive."

"I don't care! If you don't leave I'm gonna kick your ass. In fact . . . where's my phone?" Of course my cell phone had been taken from me and destroyed so I didn't even bother moving.

"You don't have to join me, Roger. But you will then have to face any impending horrors on your own. There will be more. They'll find you. They'll destroy you one way or another. This is why your therapist can't cure you. She's trying to help you think you're normal, but you're not."

"So you do know about my therapy?"

"I know a lot about you. I know this is a burden you will either adapt to or crack under. The only way to find peace is to learn how to use it. Before the next incident occurs."

Something about that hit home. I was rather unlucky and did tend to end up in bloody messes. "Okay, I'll humor you. This organization you run . . . it's big?"

"Not really. There are enough of us."

"And they have superpowers?" I started to laugh but stopped myself.

"No. This is not one of your comic books. We don't dress in capes and fly around the earth. My people simply have . . . abilities. Like you."

I looked at the crucifix on his chest. He followed my eyes. "You kill people?" I asked.

He shook his head. "No. We destroy evil. There is a difference."

"Not from where I'm sitting."

"Do you know what the Psoglav are? It's written with a P in front. Sound familiar?"

"Yeah. That word was on some of the art in Aldritch's house."

"Correct. The Psoglav are demons. Cannibals, to be exact, that live in the underworld. Their origins are suspect since much of their religious history was overwritten during the Crusades, but the basic story is that they were half man and half wolf, and they not only ate living humans, but dug up dead ones to eat as well. They did this to appease Veles, their boss, god of the underworld."

"Praise Veles."

Fountain nodded. "Marshall Aldrith and his followers claimed to be Psoglavs. They ate flesh because it appeased Veles, who in turn made them stronger. Did you know that Marshall was really one hundred and one years old?"

"He didn't look it. He looked about seventy five. So Marshall was a demon?" I chuckled.

"Of course not. He was a man. He certainly died like a man. Who knows how he looked so good at his age? Exercise, good medical care, diet."

"Yeah, well, we know what his diet was," I said.

"But then again, who's to say he wasn't a Psoglav. Who's to say they all weren't. They at least believed they were. Maybe if we were to check their feet we'd see they had paws. What is for certain is that they were deadly and evil. They were not men as you and I know the term to be defined."

"Then you knew about Marshall and those idiots before. Why didn't you stop them?"

"Believe me I tried. They moved around a lot. So many of these cults are powerful and act in profound secrecy. Not to mention I am too old to get into fights."

"You could have sent one of your men."

"I did. A year ago. He disappeared. I have never found him. No, that mission was meant for you."

Fountain withdrew a card and placed it on my kitchen counter. "I'm not going to force you to come right now. Please, think about things first. If you want to know more, you can call me at this number. I have a plane leaving in two days back to my head office."

"Where's that?"

"I choose to withhold that until I have your final answer. Then I will tell you what you need to know. I know you think I'm crazy, Roger, but I think if you dwell on this enough, you will see I am right. You have a gift. Don't waste it."

With that, he left.

I sat on the couch for the rest of the night, thinking about things, and wondering about the luck I'd had saving Victoria. If you could call it luck. I wondered again why the dice in Skinnyman's basement had never rolled my number. None of it made any sense to me, but then I guess these things aren't really supposed to make sense. After I'd killed Skinny Man, I'd thought long and hard about what makes a superhero. Are they born special, or are they made special through their unique situations? I still didn't know.

Fountain's gun had misfired. I couldn't deny that. But guns misfire sometimes.

Eventually the sun went down and I slept. When I woke, it was light out.

I took a shower and listened to the voices in my head.

Tooth: *Roger, you may not ever get laid, you dumb geek, but you sure as hell know how to kick some ass. Come to think of it, you play your cards right and you might even get some serious pussy from this.*

I didn't know if it was him really talking to me from the dead, or if I was just crazy.

I kept thinking of was the possibility that my life was really going to undergo more horror. Could I withstand it? I certainly didn't want to. For the first time in a while I decided that there are a few things I am afraid of. Maybe not men, but certainly fate.

Later that day I asked the Korean woman if I could use her phone. I called Fountain, who picked up immediately.

"Roger. Good. I was expecting to hear from you."

"You're crazier than I am, you know that?"

"So have you made a decision?"

"That depends on one question."

"Which is?"

I took a deep breath. "Can I wear my Red Sox hat?"

ABOUT THE AUTHOR:

Ryan C. Thomas is the author of several novels, including *The Summer I Died, Hissers, Hissers 2: Death March, Salticidae, Bugboy, The Undead World of Oz,* and *Ratings Game,* as well as many novellas and short stories. He lives in San Diego with his wife and two dogs. Visit him online at www.ryancthomas.com

For more books like this visit us online at www.grandmalpress.com

DEAD DOG
BY NICKOLAS COOK

It's the late 70s and Max and Little Billy are back from Vietnam trying to mind their own business when they stumble onto the murder of a local boy. With organized crime and local thugs on their trail, it's up to these two local heroes to solve the murder.

ISBN: 978-1937727246

WALKING SHADOW
by Clifford Royal Johns

Benny tries to ignore the payment-overdue messages he keeps getting from "Forget What?," a memory removal company. Benny's a slacker, after all, and couldn't pay them even if he wanted to. Then people start trying to kill him, and his life suddenly depends on finding out what memories he has forgotten. Benny relies on his wits, latent skills, and new friends as he investigates his own past; delving deeper and deeper into the underworld of criminals, bad cops, and shady news organizations, all with their own reasons for wanting him to remain ignorant or die.

Walking Shadow is a future-noir science fiction mystery novel with action, humor, suspense, smart dialogue, and a driving first person narrative.

ISBN: 9781937727253

For more Grand Mal Press titles
please visit us online at
www.grandmalpress.com

Made in United States
Orlando, FL
15 May 2023

33153145R00125